Irene George grew up in country Australia in a family where tall tales and yarns were prized currency. She writes about women, family secrets and becoming who you were meant to be. Irene lives in Sydney with her husband and their lagotto, Paolo.

Grafted. A Novel

Irene George

First published by IG Publishing in 2021
This edition published in 2021 by IG Publishing

Copyright © Irene George 2021
Nettlesanddecaf.com
The moral right of the author has been asserted.

Grafted. A Novel

EPUB: 9781922389695
POD: 9781922389701

Cover design by Red Tally Studios

Publishing services provided by Critical Mass
www.critmassconsulting.com

For Florrie

Chapter 1

When had Lillian stopped loving vermillion? When had it become red dirt? Years of stifling, burnt, grit thick mornings will do that to you, Stella thought as she picked up her mother's diary. The dust of forgotten years cloyed as her hand ran over the cover.

There can have been no joy in schoolwork being cancelled when the alternative was rolling up your sleeves and donning an apron. Lillian wrote of scrubbing away a dust storm that still rang in her ears, watching her mother light a fire for the copper in the backyard. Sheets, towels, everything pink, even the chooks having a rosy glow.

The stories weren't new but the words in Lillian's young hand, brought the tears that Stella had struggled to find. Less the mother and wife who had shielded and nurtured. Less a stickler for grace and courtesy as she contemplated bread with dripping for supper. Less accepting of her lot as she complained of the men becoming invisible, down a paddock, up a track, out bush. This was the Lillian who could have been, should have been.

Dust storms, massing locusts, bone dry dams all took their toll. Tomatoes and watermelons were other peoples' dreams, trees were stunted then denuded, recovering pastures never actually recovered.

The diary entries were sporadic, deeply felt. Ten years of life before cities and small towns shaped the Lillian that Stella knew for a lifetime as her mother.

3 February 1943

The darkness encroached on the yard, enveloped the house. The clatter of corrugated iron was deafening but even that was eventually overwhelmed by the wind. Orange turned to vermillion, coating and caking anything that wasn't covered. Mum was yelling at Kitty and me to start cleaning up long before the last of it settled.

Last year was worse - that green-brown cloud of famished screamers swept away the new vegetables pushing up from our first proper garden. Even the salt bush was shredded, only the spinifex survived intact.

It was tempting to continue reading but the funeral was tomorrow and Stella scrubbed at the corners of her eyes visualizing the tasks for the day ahead. A final visit to the funeral director then the florist to double-check that the flowers were all sorted for the morning and a last stop at the café where the wake would be held. Stella had chosen the flowers carefully. The arrangement should be elegant, no chrysanthemums, something perfumed although that would be a challenge at this time of year. Lillian had a clear code. There was a right way to do things. Proper china, sitting down together for dinner, napkins, a tablecloth, thank you cards – it was a long list.

Stella was shivering as she walked to the family car, chrome still shiny although it must have been twenty years old. Her father, David, had bought it when he retired and it was his pride and joy but even high end European luxury fades. The grass cracked under her feet. The early frost, a reminder of all those frozen mornings taking the bus to school, sitting on top of the tiny heater, courting chilblains. Perhaps she should have driven up from the city when the call came through that Lillian had taken a turn for the worse. The train had seemed sensible, no time to lose and no head space to concentrate on traffic. Now she would have been happier in her own car.

Still the old one was reliable and as she passed the bulk of the pine-shadowed church, she was glad of its efficient heater. There was no sun this morning. A black frost Lillian would have said and Stella imagined her making her morning coffee and settling down to scan the local paper. Lately she had needed more care, women to shower her, someone to prepare lunch, a nurse to check on the dressings. Strange that days full of appointments and visitors could be so empty. David's death sat heavily with her for every one of the four years she survived him.

Turning from thoughts of her mother to check her rear view mirror, Stella parked in front of the funeral directors and gathered the bag of clothes. Lillian's last outfit. She had thought it would be a daunting task but in the end it had come down to the practicality of what still fit after the savages of cancer. The teal blue dress had been a favourite. No jewellery, Lillian had never worn much. And shoes. She had brought the low black slingbacks that Lillian adored—a final birthday present from David. He had bought her a new pair of shoes every birthday for fifty years, always from the best department store in the city and in latter years hardly worn.

After depositing the clothes, signing yet another cheque, agreeing on the beech wooden coffin and handing over the small selection of photos for the church booklet, Stella was seriously in need of coffee. The spread of hipster baristas had thankfully made its way to this small town and she sat with a double shot latte and watched the world go by for a while. Well actually, not much went by, the cold morning was an excuse for a sleepy start in this part of the world.

Two women came down the steps of the church, bucket and mop in hand. Preparing for tomorrow no doubt. The baker across the street was busy – young fellows in their high vis vests and sturdy work boots dropping in for meat pies and mums with toddlers trying to stymy a tantrum with the promise of cake. The coffee shop's regulars were in for a quick takeaway. A few words about the weather and they were off to work. Out the back Stella could see someone making sandwiches and rolls ready for the lunch time crowd. Reaching into her bag, she pulled out the list, already slightly crumped.

The priest was coming to the house at 11am. There was the eulogy to review one final time and photos to be chosen for the wake. Stella had spent much of the previous night cleaning, methodically taking back control. Ticking it off the list now brought a return of that calm. All the family and friends had been notified and the network of cousins ensured no acquaintance was forgotten. She had cancelled all the carers, nurses and medical appointments. The list of upcoming appointments on the fridge also mentioned one for a podiatrist but she didn't have a name or number. Perhaps the doctors' surgery could help with that one. Finishing the last of her coffee, Stella grimaced at the time- she would have the priest waiting on the doorstep if she didn't get a wriggle on.

The house, it had not been home for a long time, welcomed her back with an empty chill. On the surface not much had changed since her childhood. The furnishings were older and the garden barer but it was the stillness that shouted to her that she did not belong. She had been the one to create distance -unconsciously at first, then deliberately. It had been easy to blame her parents, to tell her friends that her family did not understand her life, but Stella knew that was down to her. How could they understand what she never told?

Stella had thought a lot about her years living in this town over the past few days. She had been bright and competitive, not traits the popular girls valued. She remembered the father of a classmate asking her at the school graduation why she was wasting her father's money going to university when she could easily get a job in the bank. She wondered what he would say now that the last bank in town had closed.

David had loved this town and was proud of the three generations who had lived there. It was his place, deep in his blood. Lillian had been glad of its conveniences after her outback life but she had also missed the city of her twenties. As a young bride, the locals had been wary of her and when she produced a daughter who talked about travelling and tertiary study the school mothers became unwelcoming at best. There was gossip that she thought she was better than them with her carefully set hair, manicured nails and one nice frock for good. Stella, like her mother, knew that acceptance was not a price you could pay for their type of ordinariness.

Lillian had finally found her tribe at the local dramatic society and with a land care group that volunteered to weed the local bushland. She and her sister Kitty were close and saw a lot of each other until Kitty died when Stella was still young. After Stella had left school, Lillian volunteered to help students with their reading on Wednesday afternoons. She and the head teacher became friendly and often went to the city together for a day of shopping in the school holidays.

Father Michael arrived a few minutes after she drove into the yard. Short, slightly disheveled, he was in need of a hair cut and a pair of pants that fit properly. Her smelt like that jacket at the back of the cupboard that you really should have had dry cleaned before you hung it at the end of last winter. Not exactly dirty but a long time since it had been fresh. Lillian had been a regular church goer and David had had a deep faith. Stella always suspected that Lillian had found stillness and reassurance in the church more readily than god but they had never discussed it. As a child and adolescent, Stella had gone to mass with her parents most Sundays and so selecting readings for the service was straightforward. Love, tolerance, resilience, gratitude – those were traits that she associated with Lillian and that she knew Lillian valued in others. Should she make a donation to the church? It would be appreciated of course but no obligation. The church choir was available, a selection of requiem standards, some of Lillian's favorite songs as the coffin was lowered into the ground, cousins and friends named to read and officiate – more decisions ticked off the list.

Stella sifted and scanned photos all afternoon, well after she needed to turn the lights on and the heating up. How often as a child had she pawed over the old black photo album with its heavy pages and fiddly photo corners that predated Lillian's marriage to David? Tiny box brownie images, faded places, blurred memories. Luckily, she had sat with Lillian years earlier and added captions, otherwise many faces would have remained nameless forever. She chose photos from when Lillian was a girl, growing up in the far west, with her parents on the farm and later at the pub. There were the debutante photos from her first formal dance, maybe in Nyngan and later skylarking with her girl friends in the city—dance halls, picnics and tennis matches.

Her mum had not been beautiful, classically or otherwise. But she'd had style and poise and she was always immaculately groomed. The only things Lillian had hated about her time working at the telephone exchange in the city had been the way the headsets had spoilt her hairdo. She never had lots of clothes but even when things were tight she chose well cut classics. Better to have one good dress that cost a month's salary and that would always look good. Back then no one expected you to have a new dress every weekend. Pleated skirts and knitted tops had been the mainstay of her work wardrobe and even as fashions changed over the years she they remained her day to day basics.

Lillian had met David when she was visiting her older sister, Kitty in her early twenties. She had taken the train from the city for a weekend in the mountains to go to a dance at the grand hotel that looked down over the steep rocky valley. There was a big band, some booze out the back and endless dancing. She loved to dance. David on the other hand was all left feet but by some inspiration he had asked her to dance and as they say, the rest is history. David was a local teacher, an only child and thoroughly decent. Lillian was the third of six siblings, practical but also with ambitions that belied her remote upbringing. Those dreams would ultimately be curbed by small town horizons but from that first dance she added a spark to life that David had never imagined.

Less than a year and many trips between the mountains and the city later they were married and they settled into a rented house while they built the small cottage that was to become home. There were photos of Sunday drives, family lunches, Christmas 1956 when they were engaged and then in Bourke for the new year visiting her parents. David used to tell a story about his first trip to Bourke to meet her parents. The drive was hot and dusty in his old Holden and they were tired when they arrived about 10 o'clock that the evening. David was desperate for a shower but his soon-to-be-relatives told him he would have to wait. It was not until almost one o'clock in the morning that the artesian bore water would be cool enough to use.

The wedding was in Bourke too. The men in black suits and white gloves looked uncomfortable and sweaty. The women wore ensembles like the young Queen Elizabeth, a frock with a matching light coat, as their makeup melted in the March sunshine. Lillian's dress had enough tulle to wrap the wedding car twice over and her four bridesmaids wore fashionable calf length dresses and cocktail hats for the midday wedding. Lillian looked more anxious than radiant in most of the photos and both sets of the parents stared without humour or malice at the camera. Not to say they were not happy with the match, just that the parched grounds of the church yard and the paddocks beyond were a constant reminder that life was hard.

Lillian had to stop work like all married women in government jobs and she set about creating a home that had as little as possible in common with those of her childhood. There were photos of her in the garden, amongst the roses, planting fruit trees down the back, feeding the chickens, even hand feeding a lamb. There she was selecting a carpet for the bedrooms and in that one it looked like she and David were testing out lounge suites.

Except for occasional holidays and Christmases, the photos fell away until Stella was born. Five years until their gorgeous daughter made them a complete family. Both her parents had doted on Stella but David especially saw everything that he loved in her mother in the little girl.

The album exploded with photos after Stella was born. Cradled by her mother at the hospital, a proud David holding her at full length, with her young cousins, with her grandparents, in the christening robe, only seven days old. Her every moment seemed to have been captured in those early days. Pulling herself from childhood reminisces, Stella searched for more photos of Lillian. There were long gaps after the baby years, summer holidays at the beach with David's cousin's family, milestone like Stella's first day of school, occasional dinners with friends, their first overseas holiday to Fiji, a family reunion of her clan in Bourke almost 20 years ago. Stella added a few more recent photos from her phone, attached the play list that spanned her memories of Lillian and closed the file without checking it.

Enough for one night. The fridge was full of offerings from thoughtful neighbours, Stella took out the homemade sausage rolls that Ruth next door had brought in yesterday and heated them in the oven. Then she went in search of some wine. There was usually something at the back of the cupboard, not necessarily a good vintage but well aged. David's colleagues had given him wine when he retired and sometimes friends would bring a bottle at Christmas but it had only ever been drunk by Stella on her twice yearly visits. David drank beer until he retired and then he gave that up even that. Lillian might have a cherry brandy or Green's ginger wine for a special celebration, otherwise it was only tea or coffee.

Ah good! There were still four bottles of non-descript red and even a sparkling rose that looked disturbingly brown in colour. Stella chose a red at random that proved to be drinkable and demolished her dinner with a hunger she had not been conscious of. Breakfast was a long time ago and lunchtime had passed without her giving it a thought. Another glass of wine, if only for the calories, Stella poured a generous measure into the crystal that had been a wedding gift. All the good glasses and china, mostly also wedding gifts, were in the glass fronted veneered display cabinet. As a child Stella had been intrigued with its contents and with the sliding doors that were always within reach and yet untouchable. She especially loved the small crystal bell that presumably would have genteelly called the family to dinner if it had ever been used. After tomorrow she would sort through it all, the things with special memories to take home, the keepsakes for family and friends and the rest for Vinnies. Stella couldn't stomach the idea of selling stuff. It was easy enough online but it seemed crass, a soulless way to mark the end of a lifetime. Stella hoped the final glass of wine would help her sleep before the big day ahead.

It was much later the next evening before Stella had any time to herself. The funeral had gone off more smoothly than she had expected. She had read the eulogy, tear-free, placed the rose petals in the grave before the dirt followed and greeted family and friends to remember a woman well loved. Lillian would have been surprised by how many people came. She hadn't seen herself as popular, that was David. Her own family had often disappointed her by not dropping by when they passed through town and her nieces and nephews were rarely in touch. Yet, they all came. They remembered her fondly, some thought about their own parents, Lillian had outlived most of her siblings. All remembered a time when life was simpler but also unrelentingly tough.

Stella's one surviving aunt, Eleanor, hugged her and said it was okay to weep but tears did not come easily. Even Schubert as the coffin was carried from the church hadn't worked, usually music was her undoing. She knew her failure to make a public show of grief was a disappointment to some, a confirmation to others. Truly, she was sad but she did not feel as devastated as she imagined a daughter ought. Maybe it would come. If it did, she worried it might take her over a precipice.

The house had been sorted, the car packed and she would drop into the solicitors on her way out of town for the will reading. Time to head back to her own life in the city. It wouldn't be the last time she visited this mountain village that had backdropped so much of her life. There would be the house to sell, bank accounts to be closed and documents to be signed but it would be the last time she would have any claim to it, she would not stay here again. She gave the old car a fond tap as she arranged herself behind the wheel, she would have to sell this old beauty as well back in Sydney.

Looking in the rear vision mirror she smiled as the curtain twitched across the street, those small town busy bodies were still at it. Celebrities complained about paparazzi invading their lives, small town folk were in a whole other league. Everyone at the pub would know what time she left, that she'd packed up like she never planned to come back, that no one had been there to say goodbye. Mrs Marney would lean across the bar of the bottom pub to confide to anyone within earshot, 'She always thought she was too good for this place. Sad really, not a single friend in her own hometown. Of course, she'll sell the house. Probably already on the market…'

Walking into the solicitor's office a few minutes later, Stella wondered if the clinical grey walls were designed to neutralize emotion. The young woman who introduced herself as her mother's lawyer was perhaps thirty five and coolly professional as she read out Lillian's will.

'Lillian's last will and testament, names you Stella Jane as the Executor of the will and its only beneficiary. Several bank accounts, a few shares and the house appear to be the primary assets but of course we will undertake a full search'.

'As far as I know, Lillian's affairs were in good order. She took some pains to sort everything after my father, David, died'.

'Let's hope so. It will mean we can finalise everything quickly. There is just one unexpected clause', the lawyer hesitated.

'Lillian has stipulated that before you receive the inheritance that her last wish is that you make a trip the western towns of her childhood, including a visit to your Aunt Eleanor, preferably before you set out'.

Strange, but Lillian had a way of knowing what she needed before she knew herself.

Chapter 2

Not like Lillian to reach a controlling hand from the grave, Stella returned to her earlier reflection, intrigued more than anything by the additional provision of the will. So absorbed was she in reliving moments of the past week that the slow weekend traffic was more balm than frustration. She reached her hand across to stroke the cover of Lillian's diary on the seat beside her, envious of the girl's passion. She wondered about her own dreams, maybe if she had written them down she would be clearer about what she wanted from life.

Not that she had anything to regret—a great job, an apartment that she had never thought she would be able to afford, good friends, an occasional relationship and she travelled two or three times a year. She may not have ever had a five year plan but she was hardly aimless. She would be lying however if she denied a certain emptiness, an aloneness that came with being the last of your line.

It was a relief to finally open her front door. She dropped the bags in the second bedroom for later, plenty of time to think about what to do with all that stuff. Tonight she needed to unwind in her own space so that she felt more like her usual self. Nothing better on Sunday evening than some Beethoven, toast on the couch and maybe an episode of *Escape to the Country* before bed. She was beyond tired and tomorrow she had a busy day with important meetings.

When she was still tossing at 2am, recounting messy lists of things to do, reliving the past few days, regretting small missteps, Stella turned on the radio. Perhaps some music would settle the twist of thoughts. Soon the anxiety of not having had enough sleep for the day ahead would raise the bar on insomnia higher, another hurdle to oblivion. She remembered having read somewhere that even when you feel like you have been awake all night that you do in fact sleep more than you realise. She certainly hoped so. She also hoped that the station would follow the unhelpful *Star Wars* theme that was drawing to its climax with a nocturne or something gentler. For heaven's sake, it wasn't only truck drivers and bakers who listened to overnight radio.

Grateful when dawn rescued her from more sleeplessness, Stella studied her face in the mirror for signs of the heaviness she felt in her body. Blue shadows, tight lines, flat like the headache that would hover all morning. Thank goodness for make-up and an espresso coffee.

Taking up position in her favourite spot on her balcony she sat with her coffee to watch the day begin. The air was clear, the sky and sea sparkled. A slither of moon was fading from view as the sunshine brightened. She rubbed her arms as a cool gust left no doubt that winter had arrived after weeks of mellow weather.

As usual Stella was making some notes for the day ahead. The scratch of pencil promised order and focus before she was beset by emails and meetings. She had kept on top of the most urgent matters over the past week but not all of the rest could go immediately to trash. The backlog of meetings would be worse—catch ups with students and colleagues who were eager to move on with their projects and were waiting for her input or counsel.

Stella's work was an important part of who she was. She had done her doctoral thesis on poor access to services for boarding house residents and their stories continued to haunt her work. Last year she had been made full professor and a recent grant meant she had the luxury of concentrating on a new piece of research on homelessness among women. Her plan was to start with oral histories, to explore what was often unsaid. She wanted to hear the voices of those women.

Sometimes she wondered what had drawn her to this area of study. She hadn't known anyone who was homeless, indeed all her experience was of stability and safety. Sure, over the last thirty odd years she must have moved more than a dozen times and being single she definitely had a heightened sense of the need to be financially secure. Perhaps she was keeping a deep fear at bay. Whatever the initial motivation, she had grown to admire the strength of people who survived the insecurity and hostility of the streets. Some endured it in anger, others with serenity, everyone made the best of what they had which inevitably was not much.

Stretching her back as she stood to face the day Stella rued the four hour drive home yesterday. She must try to go to the gym this week to stretch out all those cramped muscles.

As it turned out, the first day back at work was good. There were a few awkward moments with colleagues who, eyes-averted, offered condolences 'on your mother's passing'. Lillian would have shaken her head at the euphemism but people meant well. The cards and flowers from her team were kind but it was their generous effort to give her space that reminded Stella of how well these people knew her.

Anna, on the other hand, had texted before lunch to invite herself over for a drink that evening. Stella would be grateful for the company. A night not thinking about herself could only be a good thing and her friend was the queen of diversion.

Anna also worked at the University. She had an administrative position when they first met and later had been convinced to complete a doctorate. Unlike Stella, Anna's passion was for teaching rather than research and she was a favourite with her students as someone who, in her words, 'kept it real without wanting to be their best friend'. Stella worried that she would never achieve her potential without a more selfish dedication to research but Anna laughed her off.

Being hugged by Anna was like stumbling into a lady's boudoir – warm and moist with gardenia. She held Stella for an instant longer than usual. Silent sympathy, the most eloquent kind Stella thought, until scanning her friend's face, Anna reverted to form and gave her frank assessment. 'Have you been looking after yourself? Eating properly? That skirt is hanging on you'

'Lovely to see you too….'

'Sorry, but you look like a puff of wind could blow you away. I have been worrying about you and to be honest feeling guilty that I couldn't get away to be at the funeral. How was it all?'

'Come in and let me get you a drink and then I will tell you everything', Stella laughed.

And so for the first time really, she found herself fully recounting the events of the past few days under Anna's forensic probing. The dash to the airport, drafting the eulogy on the plane, the endless decisions about the funeral, even the faithful supply of nourishingly dull casseroles. 'But how are you feeling?' Anna asked. 'You must be missing your Mum. They say that sometimes it doesn't really sink in until weeks after the funeral.'

'Right now, I mostly feel exhausted but there's something else, as well. A restlessness, a sort of rudderlessness that makes me anxious in the middle of the night. I haven't been feeling sad so much. But there is a nagging feeling of something being missing. I find myself thinking back over the stories she used to tell and wondering if she was happy with her life. Did she have regrets?'

'You've told me that your Mum and Dad had the perfect marriage, that they were happy', Anna said.

'Well yes'.

'And it's not like you to be melodramatic. Sure you're okay?'

'Yes of course', Stella's brow frowned. 'It's weird little things like when I arrived back in Sydney, I was halfway through writing a text message to let her know I was safely home when I realized what I was doing. Those subconscious moments when I forget she has gone are bizarre.'

Slowly the conversation turned to more day-to-day matters. Anna was revising the course she taught. Her two girls had been over for lunch last week. Claire had a new job that they were all excited about. Anna and Rex, her husband, were planning a holiday to Turkey later in the year, probably a cruise. Stella made them a simple pasta dinner and as Anna readied herself to leave close to 9pm, both women agreed it was bedtime.

The rest of the week, passed in a blur of the usual busyness. The weather had gradually worsened and by the time Stella woke on Saturday it was raining heavily and looked chilly through her bedroom window. She hugged her coat closer as she walked to her car and made a mental note to advertise her mother's car online that afternoon. She was keen to have the space back in her garage especially since she may need to store some of the paraphernalia from her parent's house. First stop was the local farmers' market for fruit and veg and maybe a piece of that devine goat's cheese as a treat. Usually she bought her flowers here as well but today was her volunteering morning at the local nursing home and she wouldn't have time to go home first and put them in water.

Stella had started going to the nursing home five or so years before after an incident one night on her way home from work. She was running later than usual. It must have been after 8pm and the wind felt like it was blowing off snow. She had stopped to quickly fill up with petrol. A woman wearing slippers and a rose quilted dressing gown walked up to her while she stood at the bowser and asked if she knew where she lived.

The poor woman was clearly confused and initially Stella thought she had best take her to the police station but the garage employee said that there was a nursing home on the street behind and perhaps she had wandered away from there. So Stella had helped the woman into her car and driven first to the nursing home to ask if the woman who didn't recall her name lived there. She did but Stella was dismayed at how nonchalant the young woman who answered the door seemed to be.

'There's a code on the door and it's locked but sometimes visitors leave it ajar when they leave. Her name is Miriam. She's got Alzheimer's and she thinks she has to get the bus home so she is always trying to escape. Thanks for bringing her back.'

'How long has she been gone? It's really cold out tonight, she'll be frozen'.

'To be honest we hadn't clocked her as missing so it must only have been a few minutes. She's remarkably sprightly for her age'.

'Well goodbye Miriam, you'll need a hot chocolate to warm up before bed'. Stella said.

'Thank you dear. Will you come to see me tomorrow? We could have cake.'

And so it had started. Every couple of weeks, Stella spent a morning or afternoon at the nursing home. In the first year she only visited Miriam, who it turned out didn't have any family living close and rarely had visitors. Miriam had been in Auschwitz towards the end of the war and had miraculously been spared. She didn't talk about those times but there were regular nightmares and she hoarded small things like paper napkins and salt sachets. Occasionally she tried to steal something from one of her neighbours' lockers but usually she was happy and chatty when Stella came to visit. After she died, Stella would come and read or chat with other residents.

That Saturday, Stella noticed a new face in the communal reading room. Well actually it was his hat she noticed, a well worn, black one that you would expect to see an old grazier wearing. Not a typical sight in this inner city nursing home. The man was alone, sitting quietly, gazing out to the garden where the therapy dog was being spoilt by some of the more mobile residents. His smile was wide, if almost toothless, and his eyes fixed hers as Stella said hello.

'Hi, I'm Stella. I visit here sometimes I don't remember seeing you here before. Have you moved in recently'?

The response appeared reluctant but Stella understood that 'Yes, he was new' and that he wanted to be go out into the garden. Pete hobbled a bit as he walked, his legs were bowed and his knees were full of arthritis. The courtyard trapped the sun and Stella found a warm spot for them to sit.

'I miss my little dog' the man began. 'He's a foxy. My nephew is looking after him now. He brings him in sometimes but it's not the same. I haven't gone anywhere without him for over 10 years.'

'What's his name?'

'I called him, Bindi …. after the burr…. when he was a puppy, he was always nipping me', he seemed pleased with his own joke.

'Are you from around here?' Stella asked.

'Depends on what you mean by from' was the cryptic response.

'Well, you know was your home nearby before you moved into St Gertrude's.'

'I lived around here, on and off. Don't like being pinned down for too long but now my legs ain't what they were.'

Stella went in search of a cup of tea and a biscuit and sat bemused as she watched the man carefully measure seven spoonsful of sugar into his cup. 'You, sure like your tea sweet'.

'Only thing sweet about me. I didn't introduce myself before but I like you. I thought you were going to be one of those social worker types. I'm Pete.'

'Lovely, to meet you Pete and I have enough trouble sorting out my own problems without wanting to solve any of yours.'

'You remind me of someone, from a long time ago. Forgotten her name. She drove me home from gaol that first time. Served time herself by all accounts and then became a volunteer'. Stella waited for the rest of the story but it seemed Pete was done for now.

'Walk with me over there, will you? That seat near the camelias. One of the girls will find me when tea is ready.'

As Stella drove away she smiled at the picture of the little man in the big hat, closing his eyes against the glare. She wondered how he'd come to be there. Most of the residents were from well-to-do families or had been professional people in their working days. He didn't fit that mould that was for sure.

Chapter 3

Most of the remainder of the weekend passed in a frenzy of chores. Given that she had been away all of the previous week, the apartment was in need of more than a quick spit and polish. The bags in the second bedroom were also on her mind. Stella knew she wouldn't relax until Lillian's things were sorted resolving to spend Sunday putting away or packing for the op shop.

There was an appointment with the CEO of Mandalay Cottage Monday morning and both the website and word of mouth had convinced her that this would be the perfect place to undertake her research. The butterflies that had started with the buzz of the alarm had metamorphosed to small bats by the time she arrived at the cottage. Every detail would need to be right today. Looking down at her silk shirt and tailored pants, she fiddled with the collar ruing how prim she looked outside her university office.

The three gents, presumably clients, leaning on the front fence did not seem much interested in her either way. The nearest was an older man, portly with a shock of white hair that hadn't seen a barber in months. The food stains on his jacket which had once been part of a business suit had a history all of there own. His younger friend should have been freezing in shorts and a t-shirt but the energy expended in railing against whoever had stolen his phone seemed to be to keeping him warm for now. The last of the trio was the oldest, face of deep ravines, bent back and sagging tracksuit pants. He would have been tall once, well built - now his rounded stomach contrasted with wasted muscle and slack skin. He was the spokesman, pointing Stella to the office when she asked directions.

The day was well underway with people milling on every bench, in every corner - some smoking, some chatting over coffee, many she later discovered waiting for a shower to be vacated. A large group were gathered around a van that appeared to be a mobile laundry in the side street. Shouting and laughter kept the volume on high with a comfortable familiarity, not unlike that among her university colleagues when they gathered for a staff meeting. Here it was difficult to tell who were staff and who were clients at first, although at closer quarters her nose was a good guide.

Stella climbed the stairs slowly, rehearsing her bid. The woman who ran this place had a reputation of not suffering fools, there would be no second chances.

'Hello, I'm Stella Reid, I have an appointment to see Dr Benson', she said to the youngish woman sitting at the desk, assuming her to be the receptionist.

'I'm Rosemary Benson, it's a pleasure. Let's talk downstairs in the coffee shop. I need another shot of caffeine this morning'.

'Oh, sorry I didn't realise. I should have recognized you from the photo on your website'. The wingspan of those bats had just got wider and their vibration faster. How could she be so badly prepared?

The two women settled opposite each other at a long metal trestle table and ordered coffee. Instant for fifty cents in a big mug with Garfield grinning on the side wasn't what Stella had been expecting but it was hot and wet. The café's patrons seemed to be a mostly clients of Mandalay Cottage but there was also a young guy engrossed by whatever was on his computer in the far corner and what looked like a group of older local women having their book club meeting.

The women were noisy but Rosemary didn't seem to notice the distractions, fixing her eyes on Stella with a slight frown. 'So I understand from your email that you have a research project about homelessness. We are pretty pragmatic around here, supporting people where they are, dealing with the day to day. We are certainly not academics.'

'This work would be more like oral history taking, story telling. I don't expect that you or your staff would have to do anything extra. I would do all the interviews, make the contacts, set up times'. Stella knew she was speaking too quickly and made an effort to slow down. 'Are most of your clients homeless or living in refuges?'

'It's more like a 50/50 split. Yes, many are homeless at least sometimes. Some live in boarding houses or hostels and quite a few are now in public housing but still come to visit because they know the people here. There's the usual spectrum- from rolling temporary accommodation with no certainty, to families bunking down in their car while they search for a cheap flat, to people who choose to live on the streets'. Rosemary mouth had tightened and her frown deepened.

Message received -no more chit chat or questions Stella thought as she launched into the details of her project.

She put on her work voice as she described her thinking to date. She explained she was particularly interested in working with women as their stories had not found much voice in the literature she had researched to date. She leaned forward, her hands cupped, as she talked about her belief that only those within a community can find lasting solutions that really work for them. For this project, her idea was become part of such a community, to bring her academic lens to make community-generated solutions more visible.

Stella watched Rosemary carefully as she ended her speech, self conscious that her voice had kept rising. God, hopefully she hadn't sounded shrill. Rosemary gazed over her left shoulder, and that frown was stubbornly joined by a tiny up-tick in the corner of her mouth.

Stella sipped her now cold coffee, determined not to surrender to the temptation of looking at her watch. Not able to hold back, she went on, 'Of course I don't expect a response today. I can ....' but Rosemary stopped her with a quick gesture and a direct look.

'You are obviously passionate and I like that. What about you find that these young women have no desire for your so called solutions? Or that their health or social situation makes it impossible for them to imagine a real alternative? What then?' Rosemary's voice was crisp.

Stella nodded, 'Of course, this is likely to be a slow and iterative piece of work. Small steps, small windows of enlightenment can be more powerful and ultimately more sustainable than big ticket items so loved by governments.'

Rosemary smiled, 'You are right there are no easy answers in this place and no room for do-gooders'. Stella could not miss the freeze.

'Send me a copy of your research proposal, your CV, whatever else you think may be helpful and I will take it to my Board. Any hint of exploitation and you can forget it. They'll want to understand exactly what you mean by, becoming part of the community - romantic notions and ivory towers are the enemy here'.

Stella, nodded again, 'Yes of course, I'll have it to you later this week. Thank you so much for considering it'. Her face was a taut smile as she stood ready to take her leave. The throb of an oncoming headache promised to intensify as she revisited every word of the past half hour. How mortifying? Rookie errors. She definitely had not done her project justice.

So deep was Stella in the post-mortem of the interview that she walked past Rex, Anna's husband, almost not seeing him. He had not noticed her either she realized as he bent his head intent on hearing whatever the blond woman beside him said, a move necessitated because the woman was reaching down to comfort the screaming baby in the pram she pushed. Stella hesitated, then lowered her lids and kept walking. Something told her eye contact would be unwelcome. Curious, she watched them walk further up the road before getting into Rex's car. She would mention seeing him when he and Anna came for dinner. She didn't want to cause a scene but Anna was her friend and she didn't want to have secrets either.

The rest of the week was consumed preparing a submission for Mandalay Cottage's Board that would be convincing. Rosemary had implied that she would need to do no less than inspire them that something useful would come of this work and convince them of her genuine understanding of their client base.

Although it had been only a single visit and a brief one at that, Stella was now adamant that Mandalay was the perfect place for her research. On that first morning she had observed three young indigenous women talking with one of the staff while they waited for their laundry alongside a woman, bent at the waist from the burdens of a lifetime and another swearing loudly at an invisible husband. All of them would have a unique perspective, hugely valuable in a project like hers. The staff were generally young and there was a casualness about the place that would let conversation flow.

Finally Friday afternoon, Stella was making the finishing touches to her proposal when an email notification flashed at the bottom of her screen. Anna, of course, making sure that she had plans for the evening. 'You can't spend too much time mulling around alone at home. All work and no play and all that'. Anna was always thinking of others, Stella's thoughts shot again to that image of Rex and the young mother and there was no denying the queasy feeling in her stomach. But this was not something for email, there's sure to be a simple explanation – not that I'm putting it off, she told herself irritably

Looking at the time, Stella gave her protocol one more quick read after reassuring Anna that she had plans. Kirsten and Steve shared the office next door to her own and they often found themselves in the communal kitchen around the microwave at lunchtime. Mostly they made idle chat about the weather or the faculty gossip and occasionally they would go out for a drink after work. Steve had been married, twice, but was single at the moment and Kirsten was excitedly in her first fully tenured academic job. Dinner would be fun – much better than take away at home.

As six o'clock approached, Stella collected her things - she'd brought some work to finish over the weekend although it wasn't essential. At the last moment she had also picked up

Lillian's journal which she'd brought into work inadvertently amidst a pile of other papers. Maybe she would read some of it over the weekend.

Dinner was loud and irreverent. Steven recounted a story about one of their colleagues at a recent conference. More than slightly sozzled, she had made a bit of a spectacle on the dance floor and then propositioned one of the more senior professors. Later she had been found asleep at the bus stop by two of her students who eventually managed to get her a cab home.

'How awful. I'd be mortified', Stella said although the woman was hardly popular and there seemed to be little sympathy for her predicament.

'When I was in my twenties and backpacking alone in Europe, I had a fear that I might have to sleep rough if I couldn't find accommodation for the night', Stella recalled. 'You'd hear stories of people sleeping at the beach in the south of Italy or see people with enormous packs, just like mine sheltered in doorways to stay dry. It sounded like an adventure until it almost happened one night when I returned to London late on the ferry from France. I planned to stay with some friends but when I arrived at their place at nearly midnight, no one was home. I later learned they had moved accommodation while I was away. In those days before email it took a while for the news to reach me.'

'So what happened?' Kirsten asked.

'It was looking like a park bench but I was saved when a pretty average youth hostel still had its reception open. I was able to find a space for my sleeping bag on their dusty wooden floor. It wasn't glamorous but it was safe and warmer than outside in November.'

'I've never travelled by myself', Kirsten said. 'Isn't it lonely?'

'Sometimes and you miss sharing special experiences with someone else but you also meet some amazing people. Lots of people will start talking to you, I think people find you more approachable than a group so that's the upside, I guess'.

'Ha, yes. My first o/s trip was a Contiki tour, circa 1990', Steven said. 'It was lots of fun but I'd have loved an occasional reprieve from the crazy schedule and semi-permanent hangover.'

The conversation continued, comparing travelling war stories and near misses. It was an easy evening and Stella was onto her fourth glass of wine in no time. When she stood up to go to the bathroom the shifting floor told her she really needed to eat something but when she came back her friends had ordered a final round of drinks. The walls leaned in but what harm would another glass do. She deserved to unwind after the past couple of weeks

Later, Stella had only a vague memory of the taxi ride home. She must have paid the fare and got herself into the building and when she woke close to midnight, she was on her couch with her briefcase pillowing her head. There was a foggy image of trying to open her front door and being unable to make the keys work somewhere behind the splitting pain in her skull. The sick feeling in her stomach foretold tomorrow's hangover and the remorse that would come with it.

Chapter 4

She woke early not feeling as bad as she expected but slow to organize herself and still feeling shaky as she dressed after a long shower. Hopefully, Kirsten and Steve had not realized how drunk she was last night—guilt and shame vied for prominence as she thought back over the evening. The mirror wasn't kind either but the flushed face and puffy eyes could be partly disguised with make-up and another long glass of water would help with the dehydration.

Self flagellation was tempting but heading out to the market was more productive and definitely more painful behind dark glasses. Anna and Rex were coming for Sunday lunch and she wanted to make something special to thank them for all their thoughtfulness in recent times. She was determined to hold it together better than she had the previous night. She worried she had used alcohol as an escape and deeper still she knew that meant she wasn't dealing with her grief particularly well. But for now those thoughts could stay buried.

As she walked down the hill from her car to the market, Stella bent her head and squinted against the light. The touch of winter in the air translated to crisp apples and squeaky cabbages in the market. She joined the queue at her favourite stall, eyeing the herbs that looked refreshed now that summer had passed. Her mood lifted as she began to feel more like her normal self. Next some cheese, salmon from the fish butcher, salad, dutch cremes and finally a bunch of natives for the table. One bag on each shoulder, she walked slowly back to her car thinking about her menu for Sunday, trying to ignore the queasy reminder of the previous evening.

Later that afternoon, Stella walked into the lounge area at St Gertrude's, keen to see the enigmatic Pete again. Two women were sitting in wheelchairs not looking at anything in particular, perhaps listening to the music playing quietly in the background. There was a family visiting another old man – the woman fussing about an orange juice that seemed to have spilled and two pre-teens attached to their mobile devices.

Continuing on into the sunroom, Stella could make out the outline of her Johnny Cash look alike in the garden. Surely, he must be cold out there. It was sunny but the wind still had a bite to it.

'How are you today?', Stella began. 'Have you had a good week?'

Pete squinted as he surveyed Stella's face, 'Do I know you? There have been so many people coming and going I've lost track of who's who'.

'We had a nice chat last week. You told me you were missing your little dog. I think you said your nephew was looking after him. Have they been to visit?'

Pete brightened, 'Tony brought Bindi in this morning for a visit. They didn't stay long because Bindi kept barking at the wheelchairs. I think he's frightened of them. Can't say I blame him. Pretty frightened of them myself. They put you in one of them chairs and you never get out'.

'Well it's good to stay independent. Keeps you fit', Stella observed.

'Sorry I didn't remember you, its taken a few weeks to settle in and feel like myself. The doctor said it's normal but it felt bad. Kind of like being in a bad dream, not able to get a proper handle on it'.

'Good, to know you are feeling like your old self. How do you find St Gertrude's?', Stella asked.

'I didn't find it, it found me', he laughed. 'Could be worse. I didn't want to come but there wasn't much choice when I was discharged from hospital. The bloody social worker had me booked in before I knew what was what.'

'They don't let you stay in hospital long these days, want everyone out as soon as possible. Where were you living before?'

'A boarding house. Not a bad place, run down but kind people. They made sure I had a hot meal every day and when I got sick they sent for the ambulance. Pneumonia, terrible cough, couldn't breathe, thought I would die. My nephew is a banker, rich fellow, he's paying for me to be here'.

'The pneumonia sounds awful, no wonder its taken you a few weeks to feel normal again. Have you always lived in Sydney?'

I've been everywhere, man', Pete quipped. After a few moments apparently thinking back on better days, he started again.

'I was born about six hours drive west of here. A small town on the plains. My mother was only young, Dad ran off when I was two or three and my sister was a baby. Mum married again and Rick took a dislike to me. There were lots of beltings. He'd get drunk on a Friday night and I'd hide when he came home afraid he would hit me. If it wasn't me, it would be Mum. He was no good'. Stella made a sympathetic noise and Pete took it as a sign to continue with his story.

'I left home when I was fourteen and got a job in the shearing sheds. That was the life. Hard work, good blokes and plenty of plain tucker. I moved around a lot, following the work. Along the Bogan, on up to Queensland, back down to Bourke and Brewarinna, occasionally back home to see Mum. Rick died a couple of years after I left. Car accident. He was hit by a train at a railway crossing'.

'How did your Mum and sister get by with both you and Rick gone?' Stella asked.

'Mum was tough, you know. She worked as a bar maid in the afternoons and took in washing. I sent her money when I could. She had this throaty laugh and she always wore an apron around the house. She had these awful old black lace up shoes that she swore she could walk anywhere in', Pete stared over her shoulder for a minute, 'My sister was a real beauty, not like me. She left home after Rick died. Got lucky, met an ambitious young fellow who did well for himself in the city'.

'What was it like on those sheep stations out west? My Mum came from up that way and I've often wondered', Stella asked.

'Hot, dry, red. But the people are decent. You should go and see for yourself.'

'Hmm. Mum didn't have many good things to say about life out there although it was during the war and depression, so I guess times were hard everywhere'.

'Yeah, but you know all this remembering is thirsty work. Reckon you could get me a coffee. They won't let me have anything stronger worse luck', Pete grinned.

Stella went in search of the coffee, remembering to bring back plenty of sugar. Pete had his eyes closed as she walked over but he stirred himself and mumbled what could have been his thanks.

All attention on his coffee, the quiet was disturbed only by the occasional slurp. Stella couldn't help but compare this man's life to her own more prosaic one. She'd spent the day beating herself up about a couple of glasses of wine too many. He had faced life front-on and then ended up at St Gertrude's. There was romance in the constant moving, shifting places, shifting shapes as the fates willed but they weren't always kind.

'Were you always a shearer?', she asked.

'God no, shearing breaks a man's back. It's a young bloke's game. I did some fencing work for a fella near Cobar in the off-season and he asked me to stay on and help on his property. I had me own house there, nothing fancy mind, corrugated iron and old sleepers but I had never lived by myself. Even started to get ideas of getting married, having kids.'

'Did you? Get married I mean?'

'No woman in her right mind would have wanted to marry me. Footloose, no money. Women want a proper home, even my Mum had managed that. What about you, you married?'

Stella shouldn't have been taken aback by the question. 'Ah no, it has never happened. Never met the right person I suppose. I used to think I would have kids but that's not likely now'.

'Better off by yourself', Pete affirmed. 'No-one to complain about the state of the house. No one to blame for things going wrong.'

'Ha, maybe you're right. I don't have anyone to answer to, at home at least. There's enough of that at work and I have never been very good at following orders'.

Looking at her watch, Stella realized it was almost five o'clock. Keeping busy all afternoon had provided a reprieve from the introspection she was determined to hold at bay but it was late and Pete would be having dinner soon.

'I'll come again next week', she promised and she hoped that Pete might be in the mood to tell her some more of his story.

Next morning, Stella busied herself in the kitchen relieved to be feeling normal. An herb and tomato salad would go with the burrata. The potatoes could be peeled and read-ied ahead of the time. The salmon would only take a few minutes to cook and there was ice cream for dessert. At the last minute, she decided to cook some of the apples she had bought the day before and make apple pie to go with the ice cream. Anna had a sweet tooth, she would appreciate the extra effort.

Her hands covered in flour and pastry sticking to her fin-gers, Stella grimaced as the phone rang. It was Anna checking if she could pick up anything on the way. They were leaving now. Stella hurriedly finished her pie and put it in the oven be-fore quickly showering. She was slipping on her shoes as the doorbell rang. Punctual as ever, Anna and Rex seemed to be having an argument as she opened the door to welcome them. Worried they were early, Stella hoped it was nothing more.

'Perfect timing', she said amid hugs and the passing of wine and chocolates.

Stella hadn't seen Rex for a few months except in passing that week. He'd lost weight and was looking toned unlike poor Anna who struggled constantly on one diet or another. 'You are both looking great', she said.

'Rex has joined a gym and this morning he tells me he's going to take up long distance cycling. Middle aged men in lycra!', Anna laughed. 'Wish I had his resolve, my waistline just seems to keep expanding.'

Rex looked slightly embarrassed and wandered over to examine the bookcase. 'What will you have to drink', Stella intervened. 'White wine, bubbles, beer, water?'

Once they was settled with drinks and everyone had shared notes on how work and life were going, the conversation turned to movies, adult kids, ageing parents, the usual preoccupations of middle age. Anna always talked a lot but today she was frenzied in her attempt to keep the life in the party. Stella assumed she must be trying to cheer her up and was grateful not to have to make too much of an effort.

'Rex you've been quiet today? How has work been, busy?' Stella asked, deciding she couldn't put off her questions any longer.

'Just the usual'.

'I think I saw your doppelgänger this week. Near Mandalay Cottage when I was leaving after my shift'.

Rex laughed through tight lips. 'People often say I look like someone they know. Must have a common face. It's been full on in the office this week, no time for long lunches unfortunately'.

Anna had finally stopped talking, watching Rex, shoulders fallen, she shrank back in the chair.

Stella frowned, watching her two friends but not sure what she had walked into, she opted for a change of subject. 'Did I tell you about my new friend at St Gertrude's? His name is Pete, a rough diamond if ever there was one'.

'Oh Stella, you really should be out meeting a nice man. You don't want to be alone forever do you?' Anna was re-energised.

'Well he is a nice man', Stella laughed pleased her tactic had been successful even as she shrugged off her cowardice.

'You know what I mean, someone eligible. A lover not an uncle'.

'Anna, leave poor Stella alone. She's a saint, volunteering, and you're giving her a hard time', Rex chastised his wife. In that moment, Stella could see Rex as he would look at eighty. The weight loss, she thought. Or the weight of a secret.

'Time for dessert', Stella laughed again, touching Anna's hand affectionately, wanting to reassure – whether Anna or herself she wasn't sure.

As they were leaving, Anna hung back. 'I'll call you later in the week, there is something I want to talk to you about', she said. Stella was curious but desperate that it was only something to do with work. There was always some drama or other in the law faculty, quite the political hotbed.

Chapter 5

Wednesday morning, Anna phoned and suggested that she and Stella meet for a coffee. Glad of a break, Stella agreed to meet in half an hour. Anna was already at the coffee shop with a pot of tea in front of her when Stella arrived. She quickly ordered at the counter and was barely seated when Anna burst, 'Rex is having an affair'.

'What, don't be daft! You two seemed fine the other day. What makes you think he's having an affair?'

Pale faced; Anna recounted a series of events. There were Saturday morning calls to work, more regular overnight stays interstate, the new found interest in exercising. She had finally confronted him last night and he had admitted he was seeing a woman at work. The floozy, as Anna was calling her, was in her mid-thirties, a single mother, on her way up in the accounting firm.

Anna recounted the scene from the previous night. Rex had offered to move out. He'd been very calm. She had screamed and shouted. Nothing had been resolved. Rex had said he was sorry to have upset her but not that he intended to change anything. In fact he seemed relieved to have been discovered. No more pretending she supposed. Traded in for a new model. How could he after all these years? She hadn't told the kids yet, not ready for their reaction until she was surer about her own.

Stella let the words tumble over her. The torrent had to go somewhere and her own guilt kept her silent for the moment. She was here for her friend but she knew words wouldn't fix this.

Finally exhausted, Anna stopped speaking. 'There's something I have been wanting to tell you', Stella said. 'I should have called you last week but I was hoping it was a work meeting'. Anna drummed her fingers on the table and fixed her eyes on Stella's. 'Last week I saw Rex with a young woman and small child. I was coming out of Mandalay and he didn't see me. When I mentioned it Sunday night and he denied it was him I guessed there must be more to it. Sorry I should have told you sooner'.

'No, it's okay. It isn't as if I haven't had suspicions for a while that I've chosen to bury, explain away. I can hardly blame you for doing the same'.

'The thing is', Stella hesitated, fiddling with her napkin and avoiding Anna's gaze, 'I thought the baby could be his. A girl I think, she only looked about six months old'.

'Shit, I hadn't thought of that when he told me the floozy was a single mother', Anna sounded winded but she pulled herself upright as if galvanized by the possibility. 'My girls may be adults but they won't deal well with the idea of a half sister. I need to ask Rex outright'.

By the end of a harrowing hour or so, Anna had collected herself enough to admit that separating was inevitable. She had supposed they should tell the kids together, definitely in person rather than over the phone, maybe over lunch this weekend. Now she had to talk with Rex urgently – she didn't want surprises later. Clearly her world had been upended. Stella made her promise to call that night and let her know how she was.

Stella was still feeling shell-shocked as she walked back to her office. Anna and Rex had seemed like the perfect couple with the perfect family. It made you wonder if you really knew anyone or if any home was truly happy. It would certainly be a wrench for Anna, separating, potentially living alone. As far as she knew, Anna and Rex had started going out in high school and had married soon after Rex graduated from an accounting course in their early twenties. Neither of them had ever really been with anyone else. The prospect of dating would be daunting but presumably that was a long way down the track for Anna.

Anna called as promised that evening. Rex had already been packed when she arrived home. He had found an Airbnb for the time being. He said he had been unhappy for a while and that he didn't see any going back to the way things were. Anna's voice was flat, defeated as she conceded to Stella that her guess had been correct. 'I asked him straight out if the baby girl was his. He started to say he couldn't be sure but then admitted that she was. Mary Rose, eight months old. The affair has been going on for a couple of years from what I could gather'.

'So Sunday lunch with the girls is going to be even more difficult than I thought. Two bombshells will be dropped on them'. There was a heavy silence on the line, 'Everything is moving so quickly', she said. 'I only admitted to myself that there was a problem a week ago and now it seems it's all over. How can he have been so unhappy and I never even noticed? Or at least pretended it couldn't be true?'

Hanging up after offering whatever support she could give, Stella thought about how her parents marriage had survived the many ups and downs of life, seeming to grow stronger as they got older. What had their secret been she wondered. She remembered a colleague once saying that the reason her marriage of forty plus years had stayed strong was because of all the things she didn't say. Because of all the times she had held her tongue, as she had put it. Stella's thoughts moved to another conversation she'd had at the funeral with one of Lillian's friends from the Landcare group. Melanie must be almost eighty and she said that she was busy down-sizing, selling her house and moving to an apartment. She had also confided that her ex-husband who she had divorced decades before had recently been diagnosed with Alzheimer's and that she was visiting him three or four days a week. Other than their daughter she was his main carer – the first family as she dubbed them. Life was never linear.

That night Stella wished she could call her mother and tell her about the past week. She missed the pragmatic warmth that could make even the worst of times better. Instead she took out Lillian's diary. Neglected these past weeks, she had read only the beginning pages and now she felt ready to learn more about that girl from the bush.

Chapter 6

6 February 1943

As predicted, Dad left today. He took the camels with him because it is going to be a big drive this time, up into Queensland, to Charleville. He'll be away for a few weeks I suppose. Before he left he told me that our neighbour, Mr Butler, said that I could ride his horse, Nellie if I wanted to. She needs the exercise and he has heard I am a good rider.

Last year I won two ribbons at the Bourke show. One for jumping and one for dressage although I'm not so keen on the dressage. Maybe I can train Nellie for this year. My brother, Charlie also likes to ride but he isn't as good as me even though he's older. He rushes the horse too much and then it digs its heels in. One time last year he went right over the head of the horse and fell on his bottom. He was not hurt much and it did look very funny but I still got into trouble for laughing at him.

Tomorrow I will ask Mum if I can walk over to the Butler property and see Nellie. She a big bay mare, not young but strong and her coat will come up a treat with a good brush.

There has been a family of gypsies living near the water tank for the past week. Dad said we should be careful that they don't steal any sheep while he is gone but Mum has been taking down bread every day and sometimes some meat when there is extra. There are three kids with black curly hair. The oldest one is a bit cheeky. She must be about five and she likes to play hide and seek. This morning Mum said I should take one of my old pairs of shoes down to their camp to see if they can use them. The shoes are pretty old but the soles are still good and I have grown out of them. The gypsy woman said she would save them until they fit one of her kids.

When I was down there I saw that the family was packing up the hand pulled dray they use for carrying their things. They will be by morning, moving on looking for work somewhere. Probably they will work on the railway line, they always seemed to need fettlers up there.

I wonder what it's like always moving from place to place. It must be nice to see different places and have different jobs. Living in a tent and lean-to would be cold in winter and the nights get cold out this way. Mostly though I wouldn't like having everyone watching me, suspicious that I might steal from them or cast a bad spell.

Before he left, Dad drove Kitty and me into Bourke to stock up on groceries. Kitty spent most of her time looking at fabric and dress patterns while I ordered the flour, sugar, butter and onions that we needed. Two boys stopped to talk to us, one of them was the youngest Butler boy. I didn't know his friend but Kitty seemed to know them both. The friend was tall and handsome and he was smiling and laughing with Kitty.

Kitty looks like a movie star with her long blonde hair and womanly figure. So much prettier than my cap of dark brown ringlets and big nose. Mum says I will grow into myself whatever that means but I'm not hopeful. I bet Kitty will get engaged soon. She's seventeen this year and that boy Norm in the grocery shop is always making cow eyes at her. He isn't that handsome but Mum says he has a steady job and that's a good thing. Kitty does not seem that interested in him, she dances with lots of different boys when there is a dance at the town hall.

The twins had wanted to come into town with us and I was happy when Mum said they had to stay at home and do their schoolwork. The twins are only nine and they can be really annoying. This morning I was helping them with their schoolwork and they were both being naughty because they wanted to play outside. They were supposed to be learning their times tables but after an hour I gave up and we went to collect the eggs and they ran around outside. The boys don't look the same, the way some twins do. The Simpson boys in town are identical, no-one can tell them apart but Harold and Tom aren't like that. Harold is blonde like Kitty and Charlie and Tom has brown hair. Mum says that Harold is older by twenty minutes but Tom is the bossy one. He decides which games they will play and he is always the hero. Today they were playing cowboys and Indians and of course Harold had to be the Indian. He had feathers from the chicken coup in his hat and Tom had the toy pistol because he was the sheriff.

Stella, smiled at twelve year old Lillian's words. It would be a few years before she had her chance to head to the city. Skipping over several pages, Stella read another entry. It was from three years later and Stella was drawn to it by the little sketch of a bride in the top corner. She had not known that Lillian could draw but this was good, like a designer's sketch of the latest haute couture gown.

27 January 1946

Kitty looked gorgeous in her cream lace dress. I was the only bridesmaid and my dress was pale pink. It had a dropped waist and I had a matching hat and new black shoes. When we arrived at the church there was a crowd of people outside to see the bride and I felt shy in front of so many strangers. One woman gave Kitty's hand a squeeze as she went by and said something to her. I didn't recognize her but I noticed Dad's grip on Kitty's arm tightened and he hurried us all into the church. That was the only time Kitty looked sad all day otherwise she laughed and smiled until her face must have ached.

She was so happy to be getting married and Norm looked very pleased with himself in his brown jacket and newly trimmed beard. They are a good looking couple, everyone says so.

Kitty came back from the city two years ago to help Mum when she had the new baby. I thought she would want to stay in Sydney and even find a job there but she said she wanted to help out Mum. Eleanor is such a cute toddler and I wondered if Kitty would have her as a flower girl but Mum said she is still too little. Everyone loves Eleanor, so sweet and docile. Mum says babies late in life are a special blessing and we all know that Eleanor is the favourite.

When she came home, Kitty was different, more gown up. She didn't like it when I asked her too many questions about her time away and one day Kitty confided that the city could be lonely sometimes when you were far away from your family. Aunty Frances wrote to her a couple of times after she left Bondi but no friends ever wrote or visited. When Norm asked her to a local dance not long after she returned she was happy for the distraction and a few months later they got engaged. There was a small party at home with cake and beer. I was even allowed a small glass.

Norm's brother, Oxley was the best man. He is older than Norm and very handsome. He and I danced together after the bridal waltz but I was disappointed when he didn't ask me to dance again. He probably thinks I'm just a kid. Oxley is a property manager somewhere in Queensland and Charlie says he is saving to buy his own property. I think Charlie has a bigger crush on him than I do!

Kitty and Norm are going to the beach for their honeymoon. I've never even seen the sea. It must be amazing but I think I would be frightened to swim. It's much bigger than our dam and who knows what lurks in all that deep water. Still Kitty is excited. She bought a new swimsuit from the mail order catalogue and she promised to bring me home some seashells. They left this morning. The house feels empty now after all the excitement of yesterday.

She turned off her light, still thinking of young Lillian and her sheltered early life. Her mind wandered to the images in her mother's old album, gidgee scrub around the simple house, a chook pen carefully tended to keep out foxes, Lillian standing beside a sturdy bay horse, presumably Nellie, neck draped with blue ribbons. So far removed from Stella's life and yet strangely part of it. Stella had an appointment first thing tomorrow at Mandalay Cottage to sort out if she would do her work there. She really must go to sleep.

The place was busy when she arrived next morning. A couple of fellows were in an argument on the front stairs and the queue for showers had already formed with people waiting patiently. One young woman was sitting on the ground, arms clasped around her ankles, gently rocking and making an occasional high pitched whimper that no one seemed to mind. One of the staff recognized Stella and welcomed her, leading her into an office on the ground floor. There was some forms to fill out for the police checks and working with children checks that were mandatory for everyone here, even volunteers. Paperwork complete, a woman called Alice introduced herself as the volunteer coordinator.

She explained that Stella would be welcome to volunteer for regular shifts at the Cottage. She suggested three sessions per week, usually three to four hours each. In addition the Board had agreed that after the initial two months (a kind of probation she assumed) she could use some of that time to meet with and interview clients who consented to be part of her study. Clients would have to agree that they were happy to be involved on each separate occasion – circumstances could change and people had a right to change their mind. Alice explained that she would have to take time to build trust with regular clients and to understand their circumstances before embarking on the main part of the project. She also warned that some of the clients had short term memory issues that might mean they would consent to be part of the project one week and be violently opposed the next. She would have to take it as it came. Rosemary would write officially in the next few days to confirm the details.

Elated, Stella agreed to start volunteering on the shower desk in three weeks time. That would be enough time for all the checks to come back and for her to sort out her other work at Uni. It was a relief that the project was finally almost underway. She knew she stood out as she was leaving the Cottage, self conscious, wrong clothes, definitely not part of the place yet. When she had asked Alice for any tips on fitting in, she had said that the most important thing was to feel comfortable in your own skin. It was funny at the Uni she felt at home, here she worried that everyone could see the façade and what's more they were likely to tell her so.

Having some time before her only class that day, Stella made a quick stop at St Gertrude's. It was almost lunchtime and she pleased to see Pete's familiar bandy legged walk making its way across the dining room. She had been putting off the trip to her old hometown but finally she had set a meeting for Saturday to see the solicitor. On a whim she had decided to ask if Pete would like a drive up to the mountains. Last time she had seen him he had seemed restless and she imagined that in his place she would do anything for a brief break away. They may not have much in common but she was sure they shared a distaste for communal living and even a few hours would be a reprieve.

His response was cautious. 'You know, I don't know about an early start and sitting all that time, my knees will be like rusty old hinges that haven't seen oil in too long'. Some reassurance and coercion later and he added, 'I'll need to stop for the toilet a lot. I have accidents sometimes when I can't hold on'.

'I'm sure we can manage that', she said. There are plenty of petrol stations and parks on the way. And look I even have an App', she produced her phone to show him the toilet finder app she had downloaded a few months before when she had been travelling in the US. The technology did not convince Pete but Stella's kindness did and he agreed to the outing. He would be ready at 8 o'clock.

Stella stopped at the office on her way out to ask what forms she would need to fill out before taking Pete with her on Saturday. She had thought she may need some sort of permission but it seemed to be a straightforward process.,

The helpful staff member said that Pete always had breakfast early and they could give her some continence pads if she thought she needed them. She hastened to reassure them that wouldn't be necessary, not sure that either she or Pete would be up for her helping him to toilet. Crossing her fingers that she would be able to manage without any mishaps she headed out to the car smiling, pleased that she would have Pete's company.

That evening Stella delved into Lillian's diary again, flipping to the entries immediately following Kitty's wedding. The weekend would bring her closer to 'closure' as they say, at least in a legal sense but the more she read, the more she realized that there was a side to Lillian that she hadn't known. Sure, she had heard the stories, some of them many, many times and she'd seen photographs but the voice in the diary gave life to those times. She 'got' for the first time how very far removed that world was from her own comfortable, suburban one.

1 March 1946

I couldn't sleep after Kitty and Norm left. The wedding is THE most exciting thing I have ever been to. The

gymkhana last year was amazing and the twin's baptism when I was little was good too. But a wedding and to be part of it – I still have goose bumps. While I was trying to go to sleep, I imagined my wedding. I will have the most amazing dress. It will be made of lace and have tiny pearl buttons down the back and on the sleeves and the longest train so that it stretches down the aisle like a queen's gown.

If I get married when I am 20 like Kitty, that is only 5 years away and I don't even know any boys yet. Charlie has a few friends but they are 'no-hopers' according to Mum. It's not that she doesn't like them, she thinks they're decent enough. It's just that they don't have regular work and some of them drink on the weekends and spend all their money at the races on Saturday. I thought about all the boys I know and none of them is smart or handsome or even very funny. Maybe once I am older, I will meet someone like Oxley again.

Before, when I was supposed to be going to sleep, I could hear Mum and Dad talking and their voices seemed louder than usual. I listened harder and could tell that they were arguing about something. I heard Eleanor's name and something muffled about Mum being too old. I wonder if they were planning to send her to boarding school. I would so love to go to boarding school but there is never enough money and now that I am older it would have to be far away. If I keep doing my correspondence lessons, I could matriculate but most jobs around here don't need more than an average amount of schooling. If I can learn to type and take shorthand, I could get a city job when I'm old enough. I will ask Mum if I can learn.

This morning I rode Nellie for a while. We practiced some jumps for an hour or two until the sun was too hot. It's been a baking summer and when we drove into town after lunch Dad was worrying that the dam will run dry. He gets most of his money from letting stock on the drove down from Queensland camp for a night and usually there is plenty of water. There hasn't been much wool to cart lately and he says that at his age, droving is taking it out of him. He said that he and Charlie would go put some rabbit traps out that afternoon and he'd buy some ammunition while he was in town. Maybe he could shoot a few pigeons to sell.

We stocked up on groceries. Mum said we could have some golden syrup and a small piece of cheddar cheese as a treat and Mr Henderson at the fruit shop had plums cheap. Mum and I will make jam to put down for winter. There might even be a jam tart later this week if we are lucky.

We stopped to see Ma on our way home. She was sitting out on the verandah and Pa was out back sawing something. He said he was repairing some roof shingles for when the rain finally comes. Ma put the kettle on and we had tea and some fruit cake left over from Christmas. Ma is a better cook than Mum, her cakes and biscuits are so delicious. She told me once that her secret is to be extra gener-ous with the butter and the eggs. She gave us a bag of ginger nut biscuits she made this morning as we were leaving and there was a new dress for Eleanor. I recognized the fabric, yellow with tiny pink rose-buds, the same as a dress I had when we first moved to the new place.

Mum is always happy after we had been to see Ma. I think she misses her and we only go into town once a month. It was different this time because everyone was at the wedding and Mum and Ma spent a long time gossiping about what everyone had worn and being annoyed that two of my older cousins had started a fight outside after the bride and groom left. Mum said they couldn't hold their drink and should have known better than to spoil Kitty's day. Ma just shrugged and said her sons' boys hadn't been disciplined properly when they were lads and what could you expect. Mum and Ma don't like Mum's younger brothers' wives, they think they are uppity and get above themselves. They especially don't like Kay because she goes to the pub with the men instead of staying at home with her kids. However they are both very fond of Albert, Mum's eldest brother and they couldn't stop talking about the beautiful outfit that Aunty Frances wore to the wedding. It was lemon and white, so sophisticated and so elegant with a matching hat.

When we got home this afternoon there was some mail - a letter for Dad from a lawyer and cards for Kitty for her wedding. I know Dad's letter was from a lawyer because there was a name and address in the top corner. I wonder if Dad's in trouble about something.

* * *

When I woke up this morning, I didn't know my life was about to change forever!

Mum and I made jam all morning. My job was to cut the fruit into four and remove the seed and Mum watched the cooking carefully so that it didn't catch on the bottom of the pan. Everything was sticky, I got plum stains on my dress and Mum roused on me for not wearing an apron. The twins were hanging around hoping for a spoonful of jam to taste but it is still too hot - nothing rips the skin from the roof of your mouth faster than hot jam. Maybe later they will be allowed some. We are all looking forward to toast and jam for tea tonight. Dad and Charlie spent the morning setting rabbit traps. They were dusty and sweaty when they got back. Charlie complained that they will have to go out later this evening as well to see if they have caught any rabbits, otherwise the dogs or foxes will get to them overnight.

And then at lunch, Dad told us the news. I was eating a corned beef sandwich and I almost choked. The letter from the solicitor that came yesterday was to tell him that his Uncle Charles (who Charlie was named for) had died near Nyngan. Charles had never married, a confirmed bachelor he always said, and he had left everything to Dad because he and Mum were the only family who ever visited him.

Charlie asked Dad what he meant by 'everything' and Dad explained that Charles had owned a pub with a small homestead and a post office attached. It was on the main road from Bourke to Nyngan and so it had good passing trade. It would be a good business for us.

Did that mean we were moving there? Mum says we can sell it instead. I can tell she isn't so keen on moving again and probably doesn't like the idea of being a publican's wife either. Dad said that Charlie can do the mail run and work in the bar and that I can run the post office. That clinches it for me, I'm ready to move tomorrow! How exciting to have a real job and my own money. I know I won't sleep all night.

Stella knew the story of their time in the pub as Lillian had spoken of it fondly. She had found she was good at managing systems and that she enjoyed the customers. Initially Kitty and Norm had stayed on in Bourke and Lillian had said she only saw her sister a couple of times a year for a long time after that. Around 1950 Kitty and Norm moved with their family to the mountains, leaving the red dusty plains forever. Charlie had also moved away soon after, finding work on a big station. Leaving Lillian at home with only the younger ones for company.

Chapter 7

What a brilliant morning, Stella thought as she rang the visitors bell at St Gertrude's. She needn't have worried if Pete would be ready to leave on time. There he was sitting in the corner chair waiting for her to arrive. He had a small bag with him, like the ones they used to give you on airplanes or group tours in the 70s.

'What do you have in there', Stella asked.

'Just me jumper and some of those pad things in case there are any problems downstairs – you know'.

'Yes of course, sorry', Stella said, genuinely sorry that she's been so tactless.

'And a can of WD40', Pete paused for effect, 'for my old knees'.

Stella was still smiling as she helped him to the car and made sure he was settled before taking off.

It took almost an hour to escape the last of the city freeways and start the climb into the mountains. There was mist rising from the valleys and smoke coming from some of the chimneys. Hard to tell which was which. The houses had finally given way to eucalypts and the outside temperature had dropped to five degrees according to the thermometer on the car. Unusually cold even for early spring and the ice warning would come on soon if it got any colder as they headed higher up. Stella felt her hands tighten on the wheel having inherited the fear her mother felt that first time she had skid on it when she had first moved to the mountains.

Stella knew there was a small coffee shop just off the highway not far from them. It would give Pete a chance to stretch his legs as well as give them time for the sun to warm the morning air. Besides, a coffee would definitely hit the spot.

Pete had been quiet, lulled in and out of sleep by the cozy interior of the car and drone of the highway. He chose an enormous scone to go with his coffee which he was making short work of as Stella savoured her own coffee.

'Nothing wrong with your appetite', she observed although Pete seemed to ignore her.

However, he obviously had heard her because a few minutes later, he rubbed his stomach, looking pleased with himself. 'You should have had one of those too, you know. Home cooking, nothing like it. Especially at St Gertrude's. You would never know it now but I used to be a dab hand at scone making. Haven't done it in years mind you. Warm scones, dripping in butter and a hot cup of tea. There is no better a supper than that after a hard days work'.

'Sound good', Stella admitted. 'These days we don't do enough physical work to justify all those calories, though. I can feel my waistline expanding just hearing you talk about all that butter'.

'Ah you young people worry too much about stuff that in the end means nothing. Live it up. Who knows you might have fun!'

'I'm hardly young', Stella said. 'But you could be right, sometimes I take the world too seriously'.

'Course I'm right, never doubt it' but his words were softened by a mischievous wink.

'You must have been impossible when you were a young man', Stella laughed. 'Not sure you've improved much either come to that'.

Continuing their banter they made their way to the car to prepare for the next leg of the journey. Stella's appointment was for 11am and they were in good time to make that easily. There may even be time for a quick stop at her favourite nursery although most of these cold weather plants would not survive long on her balcony.

As Stella pulled back onto the highway, Pete started on another story.

'You know why I left Cobar and ended up in Sydney?', he began, clearly not expecting a reply.

'The short story is I killed a bloke', he said, waiting to see if he had elicited the melodrama intended. When Stella stayed silent, he slowly went on.

Pete told her that he had loved the property at Cobar. It was a special place, hard country, it would give up its magic if you looked after it. When the spring rains came and green shoots began to appear, there was nothing more beautiful.

'I worked hard out there. It was mostly wheat and sheep country and there was always plenty to do. The river ran at the bottom of the property and we pumped water up to the dams and the homestead. It was my job to make sure all the equipment was in good working order as well as to look after the stock.

'In summer there were dances in town some Saturdays. Nothing fancy, mind. A couple of the lads played fiddle and an older woman, I forget her name, was on piano. They could raise a good tune too. I liked to dance as a young fellow. You wouldn't think it now with these old legs but I was a bit of a Fred Astaire in my time. That made me popular with the girls but their interest didn't go beyond the dance floor. I wasn't much to look at and I was only a farm hand, not much of a catch.

'There was one girl, though, Beth. She was pretty and funny and I took a shine to her. Even went to church one Sunday after the dance so that I could see her the next day. We went out a few times, all very innocent but her brother got it into his head that I should keep away from her.

'I had gone over to their place to pick her up for a drive. The brother came out and started yelling, telling me to clear out, that I wasn't to come back. He was threatening to give me a thumping I would never forget. He was a big bugger too; he could have done it.

'I started to reverse the truck, not wanting a fight. I could see Beth on the verandah crying, telling me to just go. The brother must have run down to bang on the truck but I didn't see him. All I heard was this low thump as the tray on the truck hit him mid-chest. He lost his balance and fell backwards hitting his head on the rock hard ground. It was instant they said.

'People round about didn't blame me, the police didn't bring charges but I knew deep down it was my fault. I killed that man. If I had left Beth alone, none of it would have happened.

'I found out later the reason he was so protective of his sister was that she had gotten pregnant a year or two before. She had the baby and it was adopted by a couple in town. I was the first fool to show an interest since.'

'But you couldn't have known all of that.', Stella said.

'That's the point. I wasn't a local, I didn't know the history. I didn't belong there and by being there I caused a man to die. I couldn't stay after that. I pulled up stumps and headed east. It took me a few years and lots of odd jobs but eventually I ended up in Sydney'.

'It's strange that idea of being a local. In some places it takes more than a lifetime', Stella said.

'Cobar was the closest I ever came to belonging somewhere but in the end, I did more harm than good'.

'You said something when we first met about being picked up from gaol. Was it after that day?' she asked.

'I wish. No I've had more than my fair share of run ins with the police. One day I'll tell you the story.' Pete was staring into the distance now, his eyes cloudy with memory.

Glad to see they had not too much further to go, she left Pete to his reverie and started making a mental list of things to ask the solicitor.

She parked in front of the main street and Pete sat in the sun to wait and watch the busy Saturday morning shoppers. Stella had been grateful when her mother's solicitor had offered to make the appointment on a weekend, saying the estate was reasonably straightforward and there were papers to sign for the house. The sale of the house had been swifter than she expected – a developer who planned to knock it down and build retirement flats, council willing. The price he had offered seemed reasonable and she was pleased when he'd suggested a shorter than normal settlement period. It suited them both to move things on as quickly as possible. Other than that there were bank accounts and personal effects. The twists and turns of life finally reduced to a five line spreadsheet.

As she followed the solicitor into her office, Stella remarked again how stark the décor was. Grey furniture, cold white walls, no frills or fripperies for this young woman. Apparently, she had bought into the practice a couple of years ago when the old lawyer that Stella's Dad had used all his life retired. Anyway, she seems nice enough, her fee was more than reasonable by city standards and, judging by the progress so far, she was efficient.

After a few minutes of social chit-chat – hadn't the weather been cold for this time of year, good to see the sun today – there were more forms to sign including the contract for the house sale and some bank releases. The solicitor explained the process from here on, what could result in delays and the likelihood that all would continue to proceed smoothly.

'There is one other matter', the solicitor said. 'Your mother had a bank deposit box in her own name. As she spoke, she handed Stella a large yellow envelope. It was of the type that used to be used for internal mail before the days of email.

'The only contents were this envelope and paperwork for a trust account in Lillian's name. I will chase it down with the bank but it dates back to the sixties so I don't think it is likely to hold a lot of funds', the solicitor explained.

Stella frowned, why would Lillian have had a personal safe deposit box? She and David had always had joint accounts. 'There was a trust account that Mum and Dad set up when I was born, for my education. It would be all but empty'. She plunged her hand into the envelope seeking answers.

There were two letters and three small photos of the type she had seen in her mothers album from her younger days. One was of a young man in uniform, the second a baby in its christening gown and last a tall rangy man milking a goat. How curious, the only familiar figure was the woman holding the baby. She looked like Kitty, Lillian's sister. The photos were faded, black and white, overexposed and damaged with time. Deciding to leave the letters until later, she thanked the solicitor and went in search of Pete rubbing her neck to dispel the prickly discomfort that remained with her.

He was waiting exactly where she had left him half an hour before, chatting to a young man and scratching the ears of a black bitzer. The fellow was speaking loudly but Pete seemed unperturbed so she assumed there was no cause for concern. She could hear him complaining about the government and the council as she approached. He was angry that someone had secured a lot of the dumpsters from which he used to forage for food. 'Perfectly good fruit and bread that the shops throw out at the end of the day. Sometimes even a barbecue chicken or cheese platter. What was wrong with letting people use it instead of sending it to landfill?' he asked.

Seemed like a fair question Stella thought as she collected Pete and took him up the street to a café. She had memories of coming to this place as a youngster with her friends and ordering a lime ice-cream soda or a milk shake if she had made extra pocket money. The one and only time she had ever tried to shop lift had been here when egged on by her friend Amy she had aimed to take an ice block from the chest freezer before realizing that the proprietor was watching her suspiciously. Such innocent times. It was a long time since she had thought about Amy as their paths took them to such different lives. The last she had heard she was in Darwin, married to a miner with four kids.

The tables were trendy zinc tops now and the manager wore the full beard of his generation but the fare was still honest and comforting. The menu had the usual eight ingredient sandwiches but it still offered old fashioned cheese toasties and headachingly cold chocolate milkshakes. Pete looked pleased with his choice a generous ham and cheese toasty and an enormous jam donut for 'afters'. Stella relaxed into the warm bowl of creamy vegetable soup as Pete told her about his observations from the street bench.

Before heading onto the highway, she parked outside the old house with its for sale sign, knowing it would soon have sold slash across it. The house had all been cleared out so no need to go in. The garden was starting to look unkempt but the new owners were not going to be worried about that.

'Are you sad to say goodbye to your old home?' Pete turned so that he could see her face as her as she told him about the developer's plans.

'Not really, I left here a long time ago'.

'You know you are lucky to have had a happy home. Can't say I ever did'.

'I must sound ungrateful. I'm not, but after Mum died the ties were severed once and for all'.

Pete slept most of the way home as Stella mulled over the day. The safe deposit box had been a surprise, her mother hadn't mentioned it when she was putting her affairs in order months before she died. Strange too that the carefully written list of bank accounts that she left in a drawer had not included the trust account although it was so old, she must have forgotten it existed. Her mind drifted to sale of the house. Was she sad that it would be demolished? Not even sentimental or nostalgic she realized. It was part of the past, that was all.

That evening after a quick bowl of pasta, Stella took the manila envelope from her bag and sank into the red corner chair with its high red back and deep cushions. She was burning with curiosity and at the same time reasoning that it would be forgotten letters of no special importance.

It was difficult to see the soldier's face but he was tall, slim, too young for facial hair. He was standing very straight, looking directly at the camera, wearing a slouch hat complete with chin strap. Stella turned the photo over but there was no name or date to help identify him. The photo seemed to be taken in a country town, going by the dusty street. There was an imposing building in the background - could be the post office or a bank.

The second photo was in better condition. The baby was tiny, a newborn - people did not to wait long for christenings in those uncertain times. The christening robe was white, long and lacy, much like other photos from the war period. On closer inspection she discerned it was knitted or crocheted rather than made of lace which would have been an expensive luxury. The girl holding the baby looked like Lillian's sister, Kitty. She was no more than 16 or 17 year old with long blonde hair, wisps stuck to her forehead. She wore a floral dress, belted at the waist which was far from flattering on her slightly plump figure but she had a pretty face. Stella was struck by the slack features and blank eyes of that young face that should have been full of warm vivacity.

The final photo was larger than the other two, from a different camera. The man was standing in a field bent over the goat and there was a corrugated iron shed behind him. He was smiling at the photographer, unselfconscious of the gaps left by several missing teeth. He had striking features - dark curly hair, a largish nose and brooding eyes. His singlet and suspenders that held rough woollen pants were unremarkable for the time yet he had a foreign air. Not unlike the gipsy family, Lillian had described in an early diary entry.

Would the letters shed more light on these mystery pictures? A sharp ring startled Stella and she reluctantly swapped the partially unfolded letter for her mobile phone.

Anna apologized for calling so late on a Saturday night. 'I figured you wouldn't be out because you have just driven back from the mountains but I was worried you would be in bed'. Anna's voice had the low register muffle of flu but Stella assumed it had been a fresh bout of tears that made Anna sound like she was talking through cotton wool.

'What's happened?', she asked. 'You sounded ready to take on the world last night when I called. Have you seen Rex?'

'No, no. its not Rex. He hasn't been here for over a week. But that's the thing. The girls have noticed and I've just hung up from Clare. She asked me outright if Dad has moved out. She knows and she said Jane suspects as well. They don't want to be blindsided tomorrow, she said'.

'Did you tell her', Stella asked.

'Not at first. I made some excuses about Rex working a lot of overtime and being busy but I eventually caved in when she told me that I was a bad liar and asked why I wasn't being honest with her. She even reminded me that I'd always drummed into them how important honesty was. Then she asked if Dad was having an affair – or if I was!'

'Well that undid me. I spilled it all out. How I hadn't expected this, that Rex had moved out, that it was permanent, and no I wasn't having an affair. I haven't told Rex yet but I expect he'll be furious. As you know, equal parenting of the girls, has always been a thing for us, even in the days before it was fashionable. And Jane, I don't want her to hear it from Clare, that's not fair either'. Anna was jumping ahead of herself in her panic.

Softly shaking her head and pinching herself between the eyes, Stella gave herself up to Anna's dilemma. 'I think you need to call Rex tonight. Maybe the two of you can speak to Jane before lunch tomorrow. Rex can't blame you for the girls' guesswork. They're smart cookies, it's not surprising that they realized something was up'.

'Yes, I know but it makes tomorrow that much more awkward. Instead of a dramatic announcement, explanations, tears, it becomes a slow burn of whys, wherefores and what's next and I don't know the answer to those questions.'

'Call Rex', she reiterated. 'You two need to plan this together, at least as much as you can. Do they know about the baby as well?'

Anna sighed, 'Not yet. That will be a whole other nightmare. You are right, Rex and I need to be on the same page. Thanks for the dose of common sense and sorry to dump it on you tonight'.

'Don't be silly. I'm always here and let me know how you go tomorrow. Good luck talking to Rex and Jane'.

As she rang off, her body hit the wall, she needed to go to bed. The rest would wait for morning.

Chapter 8

The first letter was in a large unschooled hand, the black ink smeared as though a sleeve had wiped across before it hurriedly The paper was ruled and the edge was jagged, like it had been torn from an old school exercise book. It was dated May 1942 and addressed to Kitty. Stella turned to the end to read the sender's name. It was difficult to make out and she squinted trying to read the cursive script -Bob.

Turning back to the beginning, she began to read. It was slow going but gradually she got used to the script.

Dear Kitty,

    There is a full moon tonight and I am imagining you sitting outside somewhere by its light with that far away look you have when you are dreaming of the future. I hope I am in those dreams but I know you were angry when I left because I didn't have to sign up yet. Have you forgiven me? Someday I hope you even feel a bit proud of me? We have just finished 6 weeks training up in Queensland. The boys are a good group, all from the bush and pretty capable but it was tough. I was glad to have Jimmy Butler with me, he's a good sort and we have known each other forever.

We received our orders today, sailing next Wednesday from Brisbane. They won't tell us where we are going yet. Some of the blokes reckon it will be up north to fight the Japs. Others are saying we'll definitely be going to Africa or Europe. We will know soon enough.

I started smoking when I came up here. They give us cigarettes as part of our rations but I've had a sore at the corner of my mouth for weeks that won't get better so I'm thinking I'll give them up. That should make me the most popular bloke in the battalion. I'm imagining you smiling at that, worried about my looks as usual even on the way to war.

I wish we could have got engaged before I went away but your Dad said we were too young. I know that's true but I want you to know that I am engaged to you in my heart. I'm not asking you to wait for me. I don't know what's ahead or how long I'll be away. Just know I will think of you every day and if you still feel the same when I come home I hope we can get married. I hold the memory of those last hours together tight in my heart.

Pray for me Kitty. We've been hearing bad stories about Singapore and Europe's so far away. I will write when I can. Don't give up on me and write to me if you can.

Yours always

Bob

So this must have been Kitty's first sweetheart, before she married Uncle Norm, a wartime romance. Kitty was a few years older than Lillian – 1942, Stella calculated she would have turned sixteen. But Kitty and Bob hadn't ended up together. Had she got sick of waiting? Had Bob come home from war and found her married? Was he one of the fallen who never made it home? Stella hoped the remaining letter had the answers.

It had been folded over into a small square and the paper had begun to split along the lines of the creases. It was addressed to Ellen from Albert in March 1943. Stella racked her brain, Ellen was her grandmother's name and Albert her older brother. Stella did not remember Lillian talking about him very much but he had been at Kitty's wedding, she remembered from the diary. Ellen was from a large family and Lillian had only ever talked about the two younger ones who had been still alive by the time Stella was born. If possible, Albert's handwriting was worse than Bob's, a fine spidery scribble.

Dear Ellen,

I wanted to keep you up to date with all that is happening here. As you know Kitty arrived a month ago and she seems to be settling in well. She has been in good spirits and eating well. We are encouraging her to take some light exercise each day, walking to the beach or the shops. She and Frances have formed a good bond in spite of the age difference and they are often out on the front verandah in the afternoons talking quietly. Frances has also been teaching her to cook and the two of them have been preparing the evening meal together.

This week we will take her to meet the local minister as she has said she would like to speak with someone from the church. We are not very regular churchgoers here but I know this fellow from the local area and he seems decent enough. There is also an appointment with the doctor, just a check up, nothing to worry about.

Have you thought anymore about your decision? You know that Frances and I are still very keen to help as much as we can and it would be a joy for us at this time of our lives. As you know we cannot have children of our own but Frances would so love to be a mother. It could be easier for Kitty as well, giving her more confidence to live her life to the full. She is such a young thing and so pretty, she deserves a chance to be happy as well.

Thank you for letting me know about the letter and I agree that we should not pass it on. It will only prolong the pain and it might persuade her to do something rash. She is a good girl but very impetuous as you know full well.

I hope you and the rest of the family are doing well and that the drought is not too severe in your parts. I will write again next month with more news. Try not to worry.

Our love

Albert.

Stella turned the paper over to read the note in different handwriting on the back. It was a 'to do' list.

Book train ticket, check with Ma what needs to be packed for Lillian and twins, ask Mrs Butler to drop in on Charlie and Dad, pack bag, telegraph Albert with details of train times, gift for Frances.

Lillian had never mentioned any of this. Kitty had been pregnant and Albert and Frances had raised the child as their own. Stella thought back to Pete's story of the day before, such arrangements had been fairly common. She wondered if Bob was the father and if he had died without meeting his son or daughter. How tragic.

Maybe Lillian's diary would throw more light on the mystery and how she had come to be the custodian of the letters and photographs.

The only other likely source of enlightenment was Aunty Eleanor. She would have been a baby in the forties but maybe she knew the family stories. She always said she missed out on all of that but if this was a secret, she would know what it was all about. Stories were one thing but secrets had the surface tension of petrol, they could spread up walls.

Lillian hadn't been a faithful diarist and sometimes many months would go by without an entry. Not all of the entries were dated either. Flipping through the first quarter of the journal, Stella found the right section - before and after Kitty's visit to Sydney. What could she glean from her mother's writing?

Lillian wrote a lot about her daily life and feelings in the intervening pages. She clearly spent much of her day outside, often with Charlie when he was not helping their father. There were rare mentions of Kitty usually connected with more adult pursuits, typically with her friends. Four of five years isn't much in middle age but for a twelve year old it is a generation.

The one exception was an account of a big argument between Kitty and her parents. Lillian wrote that she didn't know what it was about but surmised that the reason was either that Kitty wanted to go to a dance, probably the Australia Day Ball in Bourke that was coming up that week. Lillian said that Kitty had been going to Bourke every chance she got to see her friends. It would make sense that her parents were worried about how much it was costing because she was always wanting another new dress. Lillian seemed disdainful of this fact, apparently being more practical than

Kitty. She guessed that her older sister had threatened to leave home, maybe live with Ma and Pa in Bourke so that she could be independent.

Turning over the days Stella started reading Lillian's thoughts after Kitty had left for Sydney. Two stuck out from the usual hum-drum.

March 1943

I walked down the road today to collect the mail. There were two letters, one from Kitty and another one addressed to her. Kitty said she is having a good time in Sydney and that Uncle Albert and Aunty Frances are being very kind. They don't have their own children and Mum says they are well-to-do because Aunty Frances inherited some property from her father. Kitty has been for a picnic at the beach and she has been learning to bake. But most exciting, she has been to see Casablanca at the pictures with Humphrey Bogart and Ingrid Bergman. She said Bogart was dreamy but that the movie was sad in the end. I wish I could be there with her. It must be wonderful to see so many places and things. Life here is the same every day but in Sydney there must be new things everywhere.

Kitty didn't say when she would be coming home. She asked if there was any mail for her and if we had seen Ma and Pa recently. She wondered if any of her friends had asked after her. I will write to her tomorrow to tell her that we saw Ma and Pa last weekend and that they sent their love. I don't know her friends but maybe Charlie or Mum know some news. Mum usually bundles up some preserves or cake when she writes to Kitty so I expect she will add the letter that came today into the parcel.

Later I went over to the Butlers' place to ride for a while. Nellie is a good horse, she likes to jump and the exercise calms her down. I have started to practice some dressage for the show next month but she isn't so good at that. Today she kept pawing the ground and getting impatient with the slow pace. I will ask Dad for some tips on how to get her to cooperate better. He knows everything about horses.

While I was over there, Mrs Butler gave me pumpkin and spinach from their garden. Not my favourites but I know Mum is always happy to have fresh veggies for dinner. She says spinach will make my hair curl – heavens forbid it get any curlier! Mrs Butler must be lonely these days because Mr Butler has been working on another property and only comes home every few weeks and both her boys have gone to the war. She told me that she worries about the boys but that she is very proud of them doing their duty to keep all of us safe. The oldest one left two years ago, soon after the war started and the young one, Jimmy, went as soon as he was old enough with his two best friends. That was only a couple of months ago.

Lots of the young blokes from around here want to go to war, to experience the world and to save the country. Dad says it puts a lot of strain on the older folk who have to keep working hard on the land. Charlie's too young to go thank goodness and besides Dad needs his help. If I was older, I might become a nurse or an ambulance driver. I read a story about a girl who drives ambulances to take injured soldiers from the front back to the hospital. She sounded to brave, helping save all those lives.

The second passage was some pages later in which Lillian wrote about the weather – there had been rain- and the arrival of a big mob of sheep one night when her father and Charlie were away. She was proud that she had managed to negotiate the agistment with the drover. She also wrote that she drove to Bourke to pick up some groceries during this time but she would only have been twelve years old. Lillian had always boasted she had had special permission to drive to town when her father and brother were away, before she was of legal age but Stella had no idea she had been quite so young.

August 1943

Yesterday we all drove into Bourke because Mum was taking the train to Sydney. She and Dad decided that she should have two months with her brother and then bring Kitty back with her. The twins and I are staying with Ma and Pa while Mum is away and Charlie and Dad will be droving and working at home as usual. I begged to go with Mum but she said I needed to stay at home So unfair!

Still, its mostly good staying with our grandparents as Ma is a wonderful cook and there are always biscuits and bread baking in the kitchen. Pa can be grumpy and he is strict about us playing quietly and behaving properly at the table but he also takes us to the river sometimes for fishing.

I can go to school in town while I am staying here but I won't know the other children so I am nervous. I start on Monday and Mum said I should revise some of my correspondence school to make sure I am not behind the others. Harold and Tom will also go to school and they are very happy because there will be other boys to play with. I think their teacher will be stricter than Mum and me when they don't know their spelling or times tables but we'll see.

Before she left Mum made us promise that we would behave perfectly while she was gone so that Ma and Pa could see how well brought up we are. She promised she would buy us a present in the city and she said how nice it would be to have Kitty home again soon. I have missed Kitty but she sounds so grown up in her letters now I wonder if she will still want to spend time with me. Maybe she will want to get a job in town and then I still won't see her very much. I hope things go back to the way they were before she left.

One good thing about being in town is that we can walk down to Mitchell Street and buy the newspaper every day. There are lots of articles about local people getting into trouble with the police or having accidents. Some days there are poems or short stories that people send in. I especially like the short stories about criminals and bank robberies. On Sundays, Ma says that there is a man who gives a speech, like a sermon on the corner of Mitchell St and that everyone comes to listen.

Wondering if there was anything written about Ellen and Kitty's return, Stella flicked over some more pages and was rewarded with a short note.

2 November 1943

Mum and Kitty arrived home yesterday with Uncle Albert and Aunty Frances. I was shocked when we saw them because Mum has a new baby. She didn't tell us kids she was pregnant but Dad, Ma and Pa all seemed to be expecting it. The baby is called Eleanor and she is very sweet. Kitty often looks after her to give Mum a break.

Uncle Albert has a new car and decided to drive them home so that he could try it out. It's such a long drive that they stayed at Katoomba and then Dubbo before they arrived here. Mum brought us gifts, a lime green dress with white ruffles for me and a toy for the boys called Meccano that they can use to build things. My dress is so pretty.

Kitty has not told me much about her time in the city yet. She seemed tired after the long drive and just wanted to rest. She did not even ask about her friends in Bourke, not that I have seen any of them because they are so much older. I told her all about going to school in Bourke and how hard it was. My writing and reading is good but my mathematics is terrible. I have been in trouble every week especially when we do trigonometry which is especially hard.

So Aunt Eleanor must be Kitty's daughter unless maternity wear in the 1940s was entirely unrevealing. A plan was forming in Stella's head as those distant voices and places reminded her of her mother's wish for her to visit the places where she had grown up. It would be possible to take a few days holiday and drive out to Bourke, to the old homestead, to the pub, maybe she could even find her great-grandparents place. On the way back she could stop to visit Aunty Eleanor and the cousins who lived beyond the mountains. It would be a chance to check in with them and talk about what she found out west, as well as, a chance to ask more about the photos and letters. She would message to Aunty Eleanor tonight to give her some time to think about it before she called. She had not decided yet if she might ask her aunt any questions over the phone, she didn't want to be insensitive.

The week ahead would be Stella's first as a volunteer and eventually researcher at Mandalay Cottage. She was excited to be finally starting and slightly anxious that she might stuff it up. Being a successful researcher was as much about perseverance as skills or ideas, she thought to quell the unwelcome thoughts, simultaneously wishing for a good dollop of luck.

That afternoon, Stella started to prepare the opening questions for her interviews with clients once she felt they were ready to talk with her -open, honest, no judgments, no stigma. She knew the drill but she also knew that if she didn't reveal her own vulnerability she would meet only closed doors. Not a comfortable thought when she had spent decades building protective walls to hide those parts of herself.

Her mind wandered to Kitty's secrets, tied up in ribbon in the bank deposit box. Even in death Kitty had not been allowed to reveal herself completely. Would her mother, Lillian remain elusive too? Didn't everybody?

Chapter 9

Wednesday was going to be hectic and torrential rain was the last thing Stella needed, upturned umbrella offering zero protection. At least there was a seat on the train but that smell - like a cross between a linen closet in the tropics and a well used pair of gum boots. Her feet were soaked together with a good portion of her slacks and shirt. It wasn't freezing but the wind was chilly and she shivered as she slowly dried off in the train. Stella promised to get herself a decent umbrella next time she was in town. No more cheap emergency ones that appeared by magic at the front of every convenience store as the barometric pressure fell and then promptly flipped out, exposing a weak spine. Destined for the nearest bin no sooner than the first raindrops fell.

A terrible day to be homeless, that was for sure. Cardboard and a wet doona were no match for the slanting torrent that showed no signs of stopping. Unsurprising then that Mandalay Cottage was packed when she arrived.

It was a strange start - no induction, some loose instructions about manning the shower counter by another volunteer, eventually two staff members introduced themselves if she needed anything. The morning sped by in a whirl of giving out soaps and shampoos as young and old enjoyed the luxury of a hot shower. The only difficult task was convincing some folk that their turn was over and it was time for someone else to have a moment of solitude under the hot cascade. Stella was kept company for much of her shift by Marianne a trans woman who lived in a boarding house nearby. She was only weeks away from her final surgery and needing to talk about all the ins and outs. Not exactly what Stella had expected this morning but she was happy to provide a sympathetic ear and let the young woman workshop her anxieties. She had to keep reminding herself of Rosemary Benson's advice on her first visit – 'we are not here to solve problems, it is more important that we hear them'. Stella found the temptation to offer advice was strong and yet clearly none of her life experience was likely to be helpful right now for Marianne.

After her second morning shift on Thursday, Stella met Anna for lunch. The café was close to Mandalay allowing Stella to walk there at a dawdle while she soaked up some of the late winter sun. She was thinking about the clients she had seen this morning. One man was especially agitated when he arrived. He had wanted to use the phone to call the accommodation he needed for that night but he was having trouble getting someone to answer the phone. Only when one of the staff finally managed to raise management at the hostel did he calm down. Stella had never seen anyone go from such anger to being entirely meek and full of gratitude within the space of five minutes. The power of certainty or security she supposed.

Anna was already at the café with a coffee in front of her when Stella rounded the corner. Even at a distance she was looking better, wearing a long sleeved floral dress that was both feminine and practical, her makeup impeccable and her hair tidied behind her ears. Stella hoped she might have some positive news. Her warm smile as Stella hugged her hello was hopefully a sign of better days.

'I haven't been over this way for years', Anna remarked. 'It's so close to campus but I usually drive and if I do walk it tends to be directly to the train or the shops. The last time I was here must have been when I was still a student and the cheap restaurants and cool pubs were the main draw card. I'm glad you reminded me it's an interesting part of the city, seedy and run down in parts but always lively.'

'Ah, there is a reason actually', Stella explained. 'I have started at Mandalay Cottage as part of the big project I was telling you about. Today was my second shift and I realise I have a lot to learn before I will be able to fully gain the confidence of the people I will eventually interview. I was naïve enough to think that I would miraculously transfer the street cred I built up in previous work over to a new place which is obviously a ridiculous expectation. So one day at a time, feeling my way and keeping my eyes and ears open is as much as I expect to achieve for a few weeks.'

'Must be frustrating for you. I know you generally crack a fast pace in your work and this sounds like it will be the opposite. Still, what's that trite phrase - we all live and learn.'

A wry smile was Stella's only response, asking instead, 'How was Sunday? How did the girls take your news?'

'Yes, better than I expected after the phone calls Saturday, thank goodness. They were both shocked and angry when Rex told them he is with someone else and my acceptance of the situation did little to calm them – Mum how can you just put up with it? The implication was that I should fight for my husband which surprised me coming from two such independent young women who I can vouch have never let anyone tell them what to do!'

'Easy to be judge and jury when its not you in the middle. Most of us don't expect it to be our parents who aren't happy'.

'You are right. It was the loss of their solid support base that was behind much of their distress. Not that they are being selfish, it's a natural first reaction.

'And their half-sister, did you tell them about her?'

'That was the worst. Rex waited until the end of lunch, hoping the girls would be calmer by then. They were stunned, hardly said a word, just closed down. It was horrible. It would have been easier if they had yelled and screamed.'

'Both of then called me Monday to check that I was ok and to offer an alternative place to stay if I need it. They wanted to debrief about the baby of course. Rex must have been feeling battered after the girls' criticism though because he sent an apology to me after the lunch for the pain he is causing, not suggesting that he will change his plans but at least acknowledging that there are consequences for all of us.'

'Big of him', Stella snorted and then recovered herself. Anna did not need her commentary no matter how well intentioned. 'I am impressed how mature and civil both you and Rex are being', she offered instead. 'It's bound to be better in the long term that you remain on good terms. After all soon enough there will be weddings and grandchildren to navigate and you do not want that to be awkward or argumentative.'

'Well early days so far. We'll see how we go once we work through the financial separation which seems to be what brings most exes unstuck. I'm keen to do it quickly so that I can start looking for an apartment to buy. Having a sanctuary is important to me at anytime and I am particularly craving having things I love around me right now. You know all the things that I have starting packing up - the books, paintings, silly mementos from when the girls were growing up.'

'Yes, I definitely get that'. Stella agreed.

'Exactly it's part of being home that clutter of familiar objects, some full of memories, others randomly collected but now part of you,' Anna added.

'One of the facts about being single that people don't talk about is how hard you have to work to maintain relationships, a social life, connections and that is all fantastic but some days you also need to retreat to the quiet place where you can just be you. For introverts, like me that can be more often than is healthy. But you are the original gregarious butterfly so you will be better at it all than I have ever been', Stella reflected.

'Ha, we'll see. Let's order lunch I'm starving. This divorce business is making me eat too much.'

By the time they had finished lunch, Stella was feeling reassured that her friend was dealing with the current twists and turns with aplomb. Anna suggested that once she had a clearer idea of her share of the finances that Stella might help her look for her new home. She had an idea she wanted to live in the city centre or perhaps somewhere with a water view, but not far from her current place. Ultimately money was likely to be the rate limiting step, she acknowledged.

She considered telling Anna about her little family mystery but something held her back. There was a sense that this was not her news to share, especially as it was all conjecture at the moment. She knew that Lillian had been protective of Kitty, even though Kitty was older. She supposed her mother was everyone's port in whatever storm they found themselves with her commonsense brand of compassion.

The rest of the month passed swiftly and Stella spent time planning out a drive to the western plains. Lillian's diary was the guidebook for the places she ought to visit and local tourism websites filled in more contemporary blanks.

She telephoned Eleanor to follow up her earlier text message. Yes, of course, she would be delighted for her to visit. She should stay with her so they could catch up on all the gossip. She listened to Stella's draft itinerary and suggested a couple of extra properties or families that Stella might want to look up. Eleanor also mentioned that the Bourke Library had been very informative when she and her eldest daughter had visited a few years ago. She reminded Stella that the temperatures would be heading into the thirties now as summer approached and suggested that waiting until autumn when the days would be less brutal could be a good idea.

Stella was pleased in a way for the delay as she was keen to make headway on the research project before the end of the year. Her diary promised she would have a good amount of time to allocate to it and she was starting to feel she had a handle on the clients at Mandalay. Her student commitments were limited in the last semester, no teaching and only three post-graduate students to supervise. The only new piece of work was a committee membership that her boss had encouraged her to accept.

The committee was a cross departmental one that the Vice Chancellor had set up herself with a view to increasing the amount of interdisciplinary research done in the university. It was commonplace for people like Stella to work with historians, political scientists, even psychologists but she would seldom have the opportunity to work with scientists, mathematicians and engineers. The concept of bringing these multiple points of view to projects dealing with large societal issues was exciting.

The first meeting of the committee was the usual exploratory kind - people getting to know each other, a couple of dominant voices that the group had yet to moderate, more ideas than direction, nothing concrete but plenty of goodwill. It was a good start, she thought as she packed up her papers, provided they moved on from this phase quickly to something likely to yield results.

Pushing her chair back she jolted to a stop when she realized another of the committee members was standing there. It was the man who had sat beside the chairman and who had introduced himself as a professor in data analytics.

'Oh, I'm sorry I didn't see you there', Stella apologized as she stood up. 'Brian, wasn't it?'

'No problem, I should have been looking where I was walking. Yes, Brian and sorry I didn't catch your name'.

'Stella, pleased to meet you', she said extending her hand. 'How did you like the first meeting.'

'A bit waffly for my liking but I know it's how these things go at the beginning. What's your area? Something in the arts, was it?'

'Social science and history', she said getting the feeling that he considered these somewhat lesser pursuits than his own.

She was surprised then when he said, 'That's interesting, not something I know much about. Maybe we could catch up for a coffee sometime and you can educate me'. Taking Stella's smile for assent he continued, 'Good, I'll give you a call'.

Walking back to her office, she was not sure she wanted Brian to call but coffee couldn't hurt. When he left a voicemail on her work phone next morning suggesting they go for dinner the following night she was even less sure it was a good idea. It was over a year since her last relationship, more of a fling really, so it was time. But Brian? She had not warmed to him on that first encounter.

Recalling that she had made a resolution that year to accept whatever invitations came her way, she reassured herself that a two minute exchange was hardly grounds for a character assessment and called to accept the date.

Chapter 10

Over the next month, Stella would remember the words of her grandfather who used to say that bad things came in threes. He was usually pawing over the funeral notices in the local paper at the time to reassure himself that his name had not appeared yet.

She met Brian the next night at a Vietnamese restaurant near work. She was feeling nervous about the evening ahead but she had not been there before and had been keen to try it. Brian on the other hand was apparently a regular, the staff all coming over to say hello when he arrived.

The evening started pleasantly enough. Chit chat about their respective work, where they lived, what they thought of the new Vice Chancellor. Neither of them had been married, no kids, he was close to his siblings, liked cooking, competed in triathlons. Brian offered to order for both of them and although Stella thought it odd, she agreed, hoping it was a mark of old fashion courtesy.

After an hour and a half, Stella sat with her coffee while Brian disappeared to the bathroom. Well she certainly knew a lot more about him than he did about her, she thought. Not only did she know his views on contentious matters - politics, right of right; religion, for morons, and the university, full of old-school academics with no idea – she also knew he exercised three hours a day, didn't drink and preferred to eat no carbs. She truly could not see that they had anything in common.

Brian, however, seemed very pleased with the evening. Stella declined a lift home in the new car that she had also heard all about, accepting the hug he offered graciously if without enthusiasm. In the taxi, she reflected that he probably had no idea that she had found him tedious at best. She would have to think about how she was going to manage their next conversation because the text message she received a few minutes later thanking her for a marvelous evening suggested there would be one.

She was at St Gertrude's two days later, visiting with Pete when the dreaded call came. She stayed sitting beside Pete as she answered after he signaled that there was no need to walk away.

Brian was speaking loudly, apparently outside somewhere, 'Stella hi, I wanted to say again what a great night I had with you. I'd love to see you again soon if you are free. I haven't felt this comfortable with someone in a long time and I'd really like to get to know you better'.

'Ah, thanks and thanks again for a lovely evening. I'm pretty tied up for a couple of days with work and I've arranged to see my girl friend tomorrow night.'

'I was thinking maybe tonight?' Brian suggested.

'Actually, I'm seeing my friend Pete at the moment so that would be a bit tight', Stella shifted her weight to one leg, 'What about one night next week?'

'You didn't mention anyone called Pete on Wednesday night. Is he someone I should know about?', there was an edge to Brian's voice.

'Pete's a good friend, we see each other as often as I can make it', Stella knew she was being cryptic and from his raised brows she could see that Pete did as well. She might have felt guilty if Brian's next words had been different.

'So what about tomorrow night? Why not invite me over when your girlfriend comes? I'd like to meet some of your friends.'

'That could be uncomfortable. She's been going through a hard time and she needs a sympathetic ear at the moment.'

'I'm sensitive that way, you know. Women are always wanting to confide in me. Besides it could be better having an extra person there to calm things down'.

Stella doubted that any of that was true but how to deflect him. He continued to insist that they must see each other that weekend and after more hedging she eventually decided tact was getting her nowhere, 'Look I'm really sorry Brian. I can't see you this weekend and realistically next week is a right off as well. Sorry but perhaps now is not the right time for us.'

Up until then Brian had seemed oblivious to her lack of interest but now he shouted down the phone. 'Another one of those bitches who thinks she's too good or too busy for a decent bloke. What's with you women? Sounds like you're already stringing one poor sod along, well believe me I am not joining that queue.'

'Look I am going to hang up Brian and I don't like being shouted at, Stella said as Pete mimed, 'Are you ok?'

'Geez, who was that?' Pete asked, unconcerned that he had been eavesdropping on such a personal conversation.

'Guy I went to dinner with two nights ago. He wasn't that rude over dinner but he wasn't good company either and we have nothing in common. I haven't been spoken to like that in a long time, since my twenties.'

'He sounded like a pig, you're well out of it'.

'You're right and yet I still feel guilty that I upset him so much. I know it's psychological blackmail but it worked and I hardly know the man. How impossible must it be for women who are bullied by someone they actually like, love even?'

'And your old pal Pete, he must be a real accommodating fellow,' Pete's tone was teasing.

'Sorry to use you that way', Stella apologized, 'And you are right it wasn't honest of me to imply you are that sort of friend'.

'Don't worry about me. I'm flattered but I could tell that you felt uncomfortable from the time the call started. Promise me you won't change your mind and go out with him again. He's bad news that one', Pete said.

'No chance of that now. The worst thing is that I will still have to see him at work. That's how we met, we're on the same committee'.

'Could be tricky'. Pete sympathized. And it would have been but Stella was relieved when her committee papers arrived midway through the following week they included a note to say that Brian Taylor had resigned from the group and that a replacement was being sought.

She felt like she had dodged a bullet and when Anna suggested the next night that they should both set up online dating profiles she declined for the moment. She needed to take some deep breaths before she would be ready to jump back in. Nevertheless it was fun helping Anna with hers.

They chose a photo of Anna laughing, eyes sparkling with mischief that they agreed showed not only her face but also her personality to advantage. The two women were well into their second glass of wine as they wrote a draft profile for Anna.

My friends describe me as warm, outgoing and funny. They know I have their best interests at heart even when I forget to be tactful which is pretty often. Friends and family are important to me as is my career teaching law students. I love seeing the students becoming more confident and knowledgeable. It's the same feeling I had when my girls (I have two in their 20s) were growing up and they learnt some amazing new trick like standing up. I love to travel but I'm more of 5 star hotel type than a camper and if there's good food and wine included so much the better. I'm looking for someone who enjoys chaotic family times but can also chill out watching a sunset. An appreciation of social justice, literature, world events, theatre and music would give us so much to talk about and as my friends know I'm a great talker.

Pleased with their effort, Stella rang for takeaway pizza and Anna made herself comfortable on the sofa. 'When was the last time you had a date?' she asked Stella, clearly more prescient than she knew.

Stella laughed, 'Your psychic powers are working well', she said to Anna's cocked eyebrow. 'I had dinner last week with a guy that I met at work. We literally bumped into each other after the Cross University Research Committee meeting and he rang later and asked me out.'

'And?' Anna encouraged.

'The date wasn't great, dull not terrible. He talked a lot about himself, asked me almost nothing but I put that down to nerves. Maybe he was out of practice. But then on Friday he called when I was visiting Pete at St Gertrude's and it was so unpleasant'.

'In what way,' Anna asked.

'Well he was insisting that I find time over the weekend to see him, even invited himself to our dinner tonight. I felt so pressured and uncomfortable that I implied my friend Pete might be more than just a friend. Then he got really angry, shouting, swearing at me'.

'Sounds like an awful bully' Anna said.

'Exactly and you know me, I run a mile from conflict and simply don't cope with bullies at all'.

'But you can't let someone like that put you off going out'.

'I know, I need a couple of weeks, that's all, and then I promise we can write my profile. In the meantime I will follow you vicariously', Stella smiled at her friend and refilled her glass.

Chapter 11

The following week dark clouds and winds underlined the onset of spring. The jacaranda blossoms blown from the trees lost their beauty becoming brown mush. Wednesday night Stella was driving home after her book club meeting at the local library. This was only her second time and she was enjoying the people she had met there. A different crowd, refreshingly unacademic from all sorts of backgrounds. The group had already agreed before she joined that they would focus on fiction, including the long lists for some of the literary awards, and that once a year they would read a classic. This month had been Zola's classic about the advent of department stores in Paris and the discussion had revolved around how generations of innovation ran a similar course.

Stella had stayed for only a short time after the meeting for a coffee after she overheard one of the group say that a bad storm was on the way. Better to be home and dry, she thought.

The wind was gusting leaves and rubbish along the street and the car rocked slightly as she stopped at the lights in King Street. She counted two seconds separating the lightening and thunder as big raindrops landed on her windscreen. The storm was less than a kilometre away according to the calculation her father had taught her – 340 metres for every second.

The rain was heavy and she slowed down because it was hard to see and the noise was deafening. Not just rain, hailstones were hitting her car.

Her hands and forearms were rigid, holding onto the steering wheel with all the control she could muster and her back teeth ground together as she looked for a spot to pull off the road and wait out the worst of it. Before she could find a park, a hailstone hit her windscreen entirely shattering her visibility. Then a crunch and a heavy hit, the car in front of her slid slideways with the impact and immediately there was another jolt from behind. A three car pile up the papers would say.

Stella unclasped her seat belt and opened her car door, instantly drenched. A woman was already out of the car in front of her and Stella could tell she was screaming although she could not hear a word she said. Everything drowned in the rain. She was trying to open the back door of her car and Stella went to help. It was jammed the woman was becoming increasingly agitated. Her two boys were in car seats in the back, crying their lungs out, terrified.

Surprised at her own presence of mind, she could see it would be easier to release the boys from the front seat, Stella climbed into to the car to help the mother reach her sons, passing them to her, one on each arm. They both hurried to the relative shelter of a nearby awning, followed by the young man who had been driving the third car. The woman tried to pacify the boys, Stella and the young man said little. There was no point until the noise abated something that would not happen until the sounds of sirens descending on them stopped as well.

The police were efficient, taking details and statements, the tow trucks even faster, moving the vehicles out of harm's way. The systematic routine should have been calming but Stella was too shocked to remember if it had been. She could have hurt those two little boys; it had been so close. The mother was only just holding it together and who could blame her. The ambulance people had checked on the boys first and they seemed fine. Stella had a cut on her face and the young man had some bruising from the airbag. They had been lucky she supposed.

It was almost two hours later when Stella got out of the cab and let herself into her apartment. Her legs shook with a pent up burst of adrenaline and she rushed to the bathroom feeling bile well up from the anxiety she had been holding in check. She sat on the bathroom floor until her heart rate slowed and the nausea subsided. Delayed reaction. Later, she fell asleep, exhausted, still distressed, angry with herself for not having the good sense to pull the car over earlier.

The police had said they wouldn't bring charges but noted that she was at fault for insurance purposes. The car in front and her own could both the write-offs, they were badly banged up. It would be a nuisance not having a car for as long as it took to sort out but more so for the young mum, no doubt. She had given Stella her number and said she could call to see how the boys were doing in a day or so. Remarkably generous of her, she thought, given the circumstances.

The next morning, Stella rubbed sore biceps, the result of gripping the steering wheel so tightly. The bruises on her thighs were easily covered by long pants but the pain in her neck and shoulders sent her hunting for Panadol. After a moments indecision she gave up on the idea of the bus and ordered an Uber, justifying the expense with the knowledge she had a stack of papers that she had marked over the previous few evenings that needed to be returned to students.

The painkillers had provided some relief but they didn't deaden the recurring memory of hailstones thudding against the car or the screams of those two boys. Running her hands through her hair, she couldn't stop thinking about how she could have seriously hurt so many people, even killed someone. She needed to own up to her own stress levels and the bad decisions she was making, she told herself, but without much conviction to more than let time take its course.

Stella had phoned through to Mandalay soon after she arrived at work to explain about the accident and cancel her usual shift. She felt guilty that she could be leaving them short handed but Alice reassured her they had plenty of people on hand and that actually it was a quiet day for some reason.

The advantage of an extra day in the office was that she could give her post-graduate students some extra time. One of them had commented recently that she wasn't around as much as usual and she worried that they could be feeling unsupported. She was pleased then when Laura, a doctoral student emailed to schedule a catch up for three o'clock, a relief to slip back into the comfortable role of teacher and mentor.

Laura was towards the end of her third year in what would be a four year program. Her research was progressing well, a star performer, she had already published five papers. Stella would offer to recommend her for a prestigious post-doctoral position when the time came.

It was a surprise then to see uncharacteristic circles under Laura's eyes and an unnatural hesitancy to make eye contact. She was an older student, in her late thirties and her maturity and life experience usually made her confident in student – supervisor interactions. Today, her face and shoulders were taut.

'Laura, come in. How have you been? How's the work going?', Stella welcomed.

'The research is going really well. I have finished analysing most of the data and I should be ready to present it to you in the next week or so'.

'That's great. You'll be able to start writing up your thesis by Christmas if the analysis is all okay.'

Laura shook her head, 'I don't think that it is going to be possible. I am in a situation that I need to talk to you about.'

Stella frowned but gestured for her to continue. 'Unfortunately I am going to have to discontinue my candidature', Laura went on. 'No please, I need to finish this she added', as Stella opened her mouth to protest.

'The situation is personal and long standing. As you know I did my undergraduate degree in Melbourne as a mature student. I had supported my husband through his degree and once he had a good job, I was able to enrol myself. Andre had been very stressed while he was studying and could be difficult to please but once he started working everything improved. I was doing well in my studies, averaging distinctions and loving the course.

I made a few friends and sometimes we would have a drink or meal after class. Andre was often late home so there seemed no harm in having a social life apart from him.

One evening he came home early and I was still at university. I had a late class that day and we had a group project due the following week. Three of us had met to work on the project after class and although we usually chose the library, this day was warm and we sat outside at the union bar instead.

By the time I arrived home, Andre was ropeable, pacing up and down the kitchen demanding to know where I had been. I had never seen him so angry. To make matters worse a fellow student, a guy, had dropped me home and Andre had seen him drive away. He started to accuse me of being unfaithful, of taking him for an idiot while he slaved away to put food on the table.

There was a lot of yelling from both of us as I told him he was talking a lot of rubbish and reminded him that I had supported his studies and he continued to sling the most abhorrent insults. At one point he spat in my face and I retaliated by slapping him. It wasn't pretty but I did not expect his reaction. He reached into the kitchen drawer and came at me with a knife'.

'Oh my God, Laura, that's awful'.

'It was terrifying. He slashed my arm and my shoulder. When I escaped into the next room, he followed me and stabbed me four times in the chest and abdomen. I thought he would kill me and he would have but a neighbour heard the screams and called the police'.

'Was your husband charged?', Stella asked.

'Yes, he has been in prison for eight years. I had a call from the police yesterday to tell me he will be released on parole within the month. I need to disappear, overseas, somewhere that he can't find me.'

'You don't think he is rehabilitated?'

'Hardly, when he signed the divorce papers which he did against his will he included a note between the signed pages. It said, 'I will kill you, you dirty slut'.

'What do the police say? Can't they offer you protection?', Stella was finding it hard to reconcile this story with the woman she knew.

'They can provide some surveillance and his terms of parole will forbid him being within a certain proximity of my residence. At the end of the day however, the detective I spoke with said there were no guarantees. His advice was to make myself difficult to find.'

'What, you mean change your name, move away, that sort of thing?'

'Exactly. I've been dreading this for years but I have decided. I will change my name and move to Europe. I have distant relatives in Germany and I speak the language. I was hoping you might be able to connect me with a good university and supervisor there'.

'Yes, of course. Let me think about it for a few days', Stella was feeling winded. She had no idea how Laura could be so calm and matter-of-fact.

'You have been the most amazing supervisor and I hate having to discontinue here. There just isn't an option of staying. Even if Andre doesn't come after me, I will live in terror that he might. I probably still will but at least I am reducing the odds of him finding me. And he won't be able to get a passport until his probation has ended'.

'What about the University, can we do anything to help cover up your recent whereabouts?'

'I have been in contact with Student Services and the advice was to have my solicitor talk with their general counsel. They seemed confident that some type of extraordinary measures would be possible.'

Stella asked a few more questions, offered any type of help that she may need, assured her of her discretion and ultimately said goodbye feeling hopelessly inadequate. She also felt uneasy that this fellow may find her in his search for Laura, and at the same time guilty for her own selfishness.

This third conspiracy of fate was bewildering - Brian had been a passing ship, albeit with a nasty one, the accident had been resolved with inconvenience and insurance payouts but

Laura's news was devastating. Impossible to imagine how she would be able to find security and peace after such violence and menace.

Her own problems were mollycoddled nonsense by comparison. So when Stella attended her Body Corporate meeting later that evening to be told the building needed significant maintenance that would cost each owner almost $20,000, she was entirely sanguine. It was only money. Normally she would have been busily making lists and calculations in her head in the early hours of morning, panicking when the latest attempt failed to add up. This time she simply lay there sleepless, cold, wondering how Laura was coping, not only with the danger but with launching herself into an unknown future.

When sleep finally came, Stella saw herself walking to the local shops but in the twilight she realized she had forgotten to dress and was naked. She walked covertly, trying to hide, running across open spaces until she reached the shop she needed. Some people didn't seem to notice she was naked but kids across the road were laughing at her, calling her a mad woman. She woke as the first stone was lobbed towards her, still feeling ashamed as she shook the dream away.

Chapter 12

Stella pulled herself up, stretching as she reluctantly pushed back the bedclothes, another Monday. The last seven months had been tough, ever since her mother's death and she had never felt so in need of the end of year break. The rituals and events that shaped her year normally had been thrown into the air like clay targets, disintegrating on impact. Some time to herself was overdue, she thought as she made a quick coffee before her shower.

In spite of everything though her work was going well and she was ready to start asking clients at Mandalay to talk with her as part of her project. Well so she thought until later that morning. She had been nervous that if her interview questions were even slightly off the mark that the work would be compromised. So had she asked three women that she had come to know reasonably well to give them a test run so that she could iron out any problems. What she had seen as a consolation in a tough year turned to mortification when the women told her separately but as if in unison that the questions were all wrong - too intrusive, intimidating. Stella was horrified to get it so wrong – the last thing she wanted was to traumatize her participants further. It was also a wake-up call that maybe she wasn't doing her best work. Stress, she supposed, worried that she had not been fully aware of how much it might be affecting her.

Feeling bruised from the individual feedback, Stella invited the three women to lunch at the café at Mandalay Cottage the next day. Each had initially agreed to take part in the study as much because they liked Stella as any idea that their stories might be helpful.

Jenny, Teresa and Lucy had seen it all and not much phased them. Stella wanted to go directly to the reason for the discussion both to clear the air so that they wouldn't feel awkward and because she had a pressing sense of urgency to get it sorted. The only way she knew to shift that sick feeling of failure was to resolve the problem quickly.

'So, I really stuffed up with the interview questions I drafted. You all told me pretty much the same thing. I was being too direct, probing too hard in my attempts to get to the heart of issues. Obviously, I can just let people talk, let them tell me their story. What I am struggling with is how I ask them to imagine what would have helped provide a turning point.'

After a moment of looking from one to the other, Jenny, the oldest of the three started, 'Stella, I know you mean well but remember most of us have been burnt, mostly more than once. Don't expect that we will open up straight away. Give us time to warm up, get a feel for you as a person. Some of us like to talk a lot', she raised her hand slightly, But others are naturally more private or just plain suspicious.'

Lucy nodded, 'I was thinking about your questions and I figure what you really want to know is what happened on the good days compared to the really bad days. Sometimes shit just happens but sometimes people help it on its way. When I saw your questions, I felt kind of ashamed that I hadn't been able to deal with the shitty days better. You probably didn't mean to sound negative but sometimes I over-react these days'.

Stella liked Lucy's way of summing up her research. She needed to get a lot more practical in how she built rapport. These women dealt with stigma and prejudice everyday and they needed to be in charge of the discussions.

Teresa had been quiet and Stella thought she looked uncomfortable with the conversation. Finally she unwrapped her arms from across her chest. 'Lucy's right, you need to listen without being judgey and you need to do something useful if someone asks for your help. Don't use us.'

Stella nodded slowly and sipped on her coffee to give herself some time to reflect. She was surprised, although she shouldn't have been by the undercurrent of anger in the conversation. These women were right and their wisdom may just have saved her research from total irrelevance.

Stella thanked them for their candour. 'For being hard-arsed bitches you mean?' Lucy said.

'Yes, I needed to hear it and I might have missed the whole point if you'd all been terribly polite. What do they say, feedback is a gift?'

They laughed together as they finished their lunch and left Stella to look over her notes again. She sat there for a long time letting the sites and sounds of the café wash over her as she realized how much she still had to learn even at this point in her career. Nothing like being taken down a peg or two and these three had clearly been the women to do it. She wondered if she would have reacted with such acceptance to their feedback a short while ago. The stresses of the last few months had taken a toll but they may have shown her some truths as well.

December was one of those months that seemed to have about 10 days. There were the usual work, Christmas parties - too much booze, loud music and fancy dress for Stella's liking - gift shopping and endless meetings to tie up projects that really couldn't wait for the new year. The obligatory catch ups with friends that she had been meaning to see for months filled most evenings and then of course there was her research that had reached a point that was both interesting and busy. After some toing and froing, she and Aunty Eleanor had agreed she would spend Christmas there as she had no particular ties in the city. However, before she left, Stella wanted to see Pete and give him the Christmas gift she had painstaking selected for him. She planned to take him out for lunch to the seafood restaurant across the street from St Gertrude's.

Pete was looking more gaunt than usual when Stella arrived the Wednesday before Christmas. He said he had spent three days in hospital with pneumonia but that he was on the mend now. Stella felt guilty that she had not been to see him sooner. She hadn't realized how sick he was to be honest. The person she had spoken with at the home said he had the flu not that he was in hospital! Still it was good to see the colour in his cheeks and that he was getting around almost as usual.

'I can't believe it has been so long since I saw you. I feel bad that I didn't know you were in hospital. Did your nephew visit?', Stella asked.

'Yes, he came although I don't remember to be honest. I was pretty out of it. They said my oxygen levels were low and that's why I was so confused. Apparently one night I got out of bed and wandered into another room and terrified the poor women in there when they woke up and saw me. I don't remember that either', he laughed.

'I'm just glad to see you looking so well. It must have given you a fright being so sick'.

'Oh well you know me, as tough as old boots. I've survived a lot worse than flu. Are we still going for lunch?'

'Yes, of course. First, I have a Christmas present for you though. I thought you might like to open it early', Stella said.

Pete beamed with the delight of a young child as he took the parcel and ripped rather than unwrapped the red paper with unseasonal snowflakes. 'A new black shirt. You noticed this one was getting a bit old I suppose', he said looking down at the shirt he was wearing. 'Just a minute. I'm going to change into it straight away for our Christmas lunch. I'll be right handsome then'. Two quick sideways steps could have resembled a jig if his knees had been more willing.

Stella waited while Pete changed, pleased that he had liked the gift and as he came back out she could see she had chosen the right size as well. 'Very dapper', she complimented.

After they had taken their table and ordered – fish and chips for Pete and grilled octopus for her- Stella started to tell Pete about the parcel the lawyer had given her when they were in the mountains. 'I didn't say anything at the time but when I saw the lawyer about Mum's estate she gave me an envelope that had been held at the bank with other papers like the deeds to the house. There were photos and letters in the envelope. I've been trying to piece together the story and understand why they were important enough to Lillian to keep them securely'.

Pete cocked an eyebrow, 'What have you found out?'

'Well, not a lot so far but I have a theory. I am spending Christmas with my Aunty Eleanor, Mum's youngest sister and I am hoping that she can shed some light on it.'

'Let's hear what you know so far. Are there skeleton's in the family closet, do you think?'

'Maybe. The first photo is a young soldier in his new kit. The second is girl who looks about 16 with a newborn baby in its christening gown. The last one is a foreign looking fellow milking a goat. No obvious connections but the letters help a bit. One is a soldier writing to Kitty, Mum's oldest sister as he is going to war. It seems they were sweethearts. The second is from my Uncle Albert who lived in Sydney during the war, about a visit from Kitty who seems to have stayed with them for a few months. Some of the entries in Lillian's diary confirm that Ellen and Kitty eventually returned to Bourke with Uncle Albert drove them home. And surprise, surprise Ellen had a baby girl with her.'

'So what do you think? That your aunt was really Kitty's baby and that she was raised by your grandparents as their daughter to save Kitty's reputation?' Pete asked.

'Well that's the most obvious explanation'. Aunty Eleanor would have to know because presumably her birth certificate would cite her actual parents. Kitty got married about a year after she returned from Sydney so she must have recovered from the trauma or perhaps she was keen to put it behind her.'

'What about the soldier in the picture, do you think he is the father?'

'That's my working hypothesis until I find out more', Stella said.

'Sounds like you've solved the case. No so much of a mystery after all if you ask me', Pete said. 'And who is the goat guy?'

'No idea. I never heard Lillian talk about anyone with goats. Also I don't understand why Lillian had the pictures and letters in the first place and why she kept them at the bank. If Eleanor was Kitty's daughter and it was an open secret then I would have thought Lillian would have told me about it but she never mentioned anything – and she definitely liked a bit of family gossip so that would be out of character!'

'Hmm, you'll have to tell me more when you come back from the country. I'm spending Christmas with my nephew and his family. His kids are noisy blighters, always running and jumping and shouting but at least I will be with family. The first time in years actually.' Pete said.

'How do you normally spend Christmas?' Stella asked as the conversation moved on.

'Last few years, Bindi and I have gone to a big street party in Kings Cross. Free lunch and a sing-along, better than spending the day alone. Before that, I would be working or sometimes a mate would invite me to have Christmas with their family. After Mum died it was always a sad day, reminded me of all the things I would like to have been different in life – for her and for me. For a long time, my sister didn't want to know me, not surprising given the state I was in at times.'

'I've been wondering how I will feel about Christmas this year, too', Stella said. 'I usually enjoy all the tradition and trimmings but it will be strange with no close family anymore. Last year was just Mum and me and that felt lonely. I'm lucky I will be with extended family but I think sometimes you can feel even more alone when you are a spare wheel at someone else's celebration'.

'Exactly, that's my worry too.' Pete agreed. 'At least at the street party everyone is together in their aloneness. We should make a pact that we'll have a good time and enjoy the festivities come what may' Pete was uncharacteristically upbeat as he dug into his fish and chips. The sight of non-institutional food had cheered him up no end.

'Did you go out with the no hoper who rang you last time you came to see me?', Pete asked.

'No I followed your advice and luckily he didn't contact me again. I haven't even seen him around the university, his department is on the other side of the campus so that helps. Did I tell you I had to buy a new car too?'

'Living it up on your Mum's inheritance?'

'Not exactly, that's still not finalized. I assume the banks are holding it up. No, my car was written off after an accident in that terrible hailstorm we had last month. It was pretty terrible. I ran into another car and the guy behind crashed into me. Really shook me up to be honest. There were two little kids in one of the cars but everyone was alright thank goodness'.

' Think I was in hospital when that storm came. Don't remember it but there was some damage at the home and people said it was from hail. What's the new car like, maybe you can take me for a ride?'

'That's a great idea', Stella agreed. 'Let's walk back across the road and we can drive along to Clovelly and watch the sea for a bit. I know a cake shop there that would have the perfect afternoon tea for us later.'

Pete was looking very pleased with the idea. 'Sure you have time. It's real good to be out of the home for a few hours. Makes me feel almost young again'.

'Plenty of time. Come and have look at the new car'.

Chapter 13

Christmas Eve morning Stella packed for a couple of days in the country. It was one of those humid Sydney mornings when you felt like you needed to stand under the air conditioner to dry off properly after your shower. First there was a quick stop at Anna's place to drop off a small gift and wish her happy Christmas.

Anna was smiling and laughing as she answered the door, clearly talking to someone inside. Her daughters had already arrived for Christmas and they were chopping and stirring pots in preparation for a feast that evening. It seemed the girls had voted to spend Christmas with their Mum and Anna was enjoying their irreverent humour if not their taste in music. Rex, it transpired had gone to New Zealand on a cruise with the floozy. At least for this first year of separation there were no negotiations of who would be where at various times of the holiday.

'I have a gift for you too', Anna said, 'and you must open it now so that I can see it on you.' The parcel was large and the wrapping only just holding it together. Stella was genuinely touched - a sun hat, slightly askew in the crown, clearly made with love. Anna had dabbled in millinery for years and it seemed that living alone had given her more time for her hobby. Stella placed the broad crimson straw hat on her head and pretended to model the creation. The brim was wide at the front and then narrowed at the back and a thick black ribbon provided the decoration. It had something of the 1920's vibe.

'It suits you', Anna said. 'I thought those colours would be good on you and you have the perfect heart shaped face for this design.'

'I love it', Stella told her friend while at the same time feeling that her offering of a smelly candle and chocolates rated poorly in comparison.

Four hours later, Stella arrived in Belgravia, the small town where Eleanor and most of her offspring lived. She had stopped for a lunch break so as not to be one of those visitors who appear at mealtime without warning but of course Eleanor was immediately pressing her to have a cuppa and some Christmas cake.

'It's Ma's recipe you know. Mum's mother eventually passed it on to Mum and she to us girls. Mum said that Ma was cagey with most of her recipes, sometimes leaving out essential details so that you could never recreate the same dish. Apparently, that is what happened with the plum pudding recipe. Ma left out some ingredient and Mum's version was always too sloppy, like it could never fully cook no matter how long it boiled away in its calico wrap. At least the cake is foolproof.'

'I remember my Mum making it too', Stella said. 'I must admit baking is not one of my favourite things and I never asked her for the recipe. Perhaps you will show me how to make it sometime.'

'That's a nice idea' Eleanor agreed. 'I don't have many chances to spend time with my favourite niece'.

Stella laughed. 'I can't believe you are still using that old joke after all these years. May and Valerie are the only other nieces and they must both be almost seventy. How have you been? Still going on day trips with the community centre.'

'Fit and healthy, a few aches and pains but that is to be expected at my age. You know I turn 78 in February but I'm still one of the young ones on our day trips and I can help the older people get in and out of the bus. Need to stay active at my age and to have company – it keeps your mind working. And the grandkids of course. They really keep me going when I look after them although Lizzy's girls are grown up and her youngest had a daughter of her own last year. Anthony's are still young enough to give their Gran cuddles - the boys are sweethearts.'

'What are the plans for tomorrow? Will they all come here?', Stella looked around the retirement unit and assumed it was unlikely.

'No, no. I should have said. We are all invited to Lizzy's place for lunch. They have a big house on the property and lots of space. Sandra and her family have already arrived from Canberra and are staying there and Anthony and Kate and the boys will give us a lift out there.'

'Oh, that sounds lovely', Stella said realizing that she had no idea what her cousins' children were called or even how many of them there were. In fact she was racking her brains for the names of their partners as she'd not gone to any of their weddings and although she had seen them at Lillian's funeral the names had not stuck. Lucky, the family rule at Christmas was no presents from extended family otherwise she would be in trouble.

'I thought we might go to midnight mass tonight if you feel up to it after the long drive', Eleanor said. 'You know I'm not really religious but I do like the carols and the incense at Christmas.'

'Yes, of course. I used to always take Mum after we had celebrated her birthday on Christmas Eve as a final celebration for the day. Dad preferred mass the next morning and he would be asleep when we arrived home so we would have a slice of Christmas cake or some mince pies and a glass of cherry brandy before we went to bed late'.

'Your mother hated having her birthday on Christmas Eve, didn't she? Thought it got lost in all the other celebrations'.

'Yes, but we always made a special effort to do something that was all about her that day so I hope she came to find it not so bad. At least everyone could remember the date', Stella said.

'Did she ever tell you about her 21st birthday', Eleanor asked. Stella's shake of the head was an invitation for Eleanor to launch into her tale, her smile vouching for her love of a good story.

'Well, let's see that would have been 1952 so I must have only been 9 years old but I remember it perfectly. Kitty and Norm had come to the pub where we were living. They had moved to the mountains a couple of years earlier and we did not see much of them except for special occasions. Kitty seemed happier than she had been in ages, enjoying a less isolated life and her baby girls. Mum especially missed Kitty and seeing the girls grow up. Valerie and May would have been around four and two years old, I guess. I do remember they were very cute in their new summer dresses with those wonderful golden curls that Mum said were just like Kitty's at that age.'

Stella smiled, nodding her encouragement for Eleanor to continue her story although she wasn't sure it was needed.

'Everyone wished Lillian happy birthday that morning and there were some gifts at breakfast. I don't recall what but probably nothing too extravagant.'

'Actually, it was a mother of pearl brooch in the shape of a leaf with Lillian in gold across its centre', Stella intervened. 'I have it at home and Mum used to tell me that it was a 21st birthday present, especially when I was telling her how it would be great if I could have a secondhand car for mine'.

'I don't remember but sounds exactly right', Eleanor admitted. 'Well the day went on as usual. Mum was preparing a turkey to roast next day and Kitty was in charge of the trifle. There was no discussion of a party for Lillian or special dinner or anything, so when our neighbours invited Lillian to their place for dinner she accepted. They were German and always celebrated with a big dinner on Christmas Eve.

After she had gone, Mum went silent with that cold rage that terrified us as kids. Apparently, she had made a special cake and planned a surprise celebration in the evening but as none of us knew, no one tried to stop Lillian going to town. When she came home, Lillian was in trouble but she was also angry because she was being blamed for no one making a fuss at home. It was misunderstandings all round. Typical you know how alike Mum and Lillian were!', Eleanor finished her story.

'That's a sad way to spend a big birthday', Stella observed. 'No wonder she was always a bit sensitive about her birthday. Woe betide anyone who thought it a good idea to combine birthday and Christmas celebrations!'

'Yes, I remember', Eleanor laughed. 'I once gave her a combined Christmas and birthday gift and her disappointment was in no doubt, I can assure you.'

Stella had planned to ask Eleanor about the letters and photographs later that evening or another day but as they were talking about family memories she said, 'You know Aunty Eleanor, there has been something I wanted to ask you. Mum had some letters and photos in a bank deposit box that I have been trying to understand. Do you know about them?'

Eleanor shifted in her chair, possibly to make herself more comfortable or was it to hide discomfort. 'More tea or cake', she asked rising to take the empty cup from Stella as she shook her head. After a few minutes she came back into the room and asked Stella, 'What sort of letters and photos are they?'

'I brought them with me', Stella said. 'I'll get them from my bag and you can see'.

Eleanor took the manila envelope and emptied its contents onto the dining table. Then she walked over to a small bureau draw and took out a magnifying glass. 'I find it easier to read with this, especially when my eyes are tired. So what do you have here?'

After studying the photos, smiling a little at the one of the young woman and baby and flipping to the back of the one of the soldier, presumably looking for a date or other identification, Eleanor turned to the letters. It took her a long while to come to the end of Bill's letter and there were tears in her eyes when she did. Albert's was dealt with more quickly. Stella had the impression there was nothing in these last two that came as a surprise to Eleanor.

Without saying anything, Eleanor got up slowly and walked over to her window seeming to watch the two children riding their bikes on the footpath opposite. Stella was aware of the cicadas starting up as she waited for her aunt to gather her thoughts. She walked heavily back to her chair, glanced again at the photos before raising her gaze to find Stella's expectant one across the table.

'As skeleton's in the family closet go, this one isn't that unusual or even that terrible and yet it was the beginning of more sadness than anyone would have thought likely back when these letters were written', Eleanor began.

'Who are the people in the photos?' Stella asked.

'This one is Kitty holding me soon after I was born. It looks like I am wearing a christening gown so it was probably taken when they returned home from the church in Bondi'.

'I was wondering if she was your real mother based on the letters?' Stella probed gently, not wanting to be rude but deciding a direct approach was more likely to get a clear answer.

Eleanor let the question hang. 'Well yes, technically. Kitty was already pregnant when she was sent to Sydney. The plan was that she would have the baby there and then adopt it to a good family but Mum, Ellen, didn't like the idea of adoption and it was agreed I would be raised as Kitty's sister. Mum told me the truth when I was thirteen but it felt like someone else's story. Kitty lived far away, I didn't see her much or even know her very well. There was no magical connection'. The sadness in her voice suggested she wished there had been more between them.

'I presume your kids know the truth?' Stella asked.

'I have always been open about it, saw no reason not to', Eleanor shrugged.

'The other photo is Bill Samuels; he and Kitty were sweet on each other. They met a year or so before Bill went to war, at a dance. Bill was great friends with the Butler boys who lived not far from our place. Bill and one of the Butler boy died in Changi. Being the youngest, I didn't know any of them of course. I was born after all of that but Kitty told me about it before she died. Why don't you pour us both a small glass of wine and I will explain'? Eleanor sighed and relaxed back into her armchair with closed eyes as she waited for Stella to return with the wine.

'Well it's almost five o'clock and it's Christmas Eve so no need to feel too guilty about the early happy hour' Stella said as she returned and raised her glass. 'Happy birthday Lillian'.

'Indeed, happy birthday Lillian', Eleanor joined her, 'and in memory of Kitty'.

'So it was a common enough story I suppose. Kitty and Bill were both young. Kitty would have been 16 or 17 and Bill was about the same age. He lied about his age so that he could join the army with his mates.

'Before he left for war, Bill asked Kitty to marry him and she agreed but when Bill asked our parents, they said she was too young and wouldn't give their consent. Ellen said they would have to wait a year and they could write to each other in the meantime. Kitty was furious but Bill was resigned. He understood that her parents were being protective and he could wait until his first home leave or the end of the war whichever happened first.'

'But Bill didn't come back did he. That's sad. But I read in Lillian's diary that Kitty was married when she was 20 years old to Norm. Is that right?', Stella asked.

'Well yes but not before life intervened. You see about a month after Bill left, Kitty realized she was pregnant. She didn't tell anyone immediately but eventually she told Mum. As you know, Ellen was very Catholic and she would have been mortified but ever practical, she arranged for Kitty to go to Sydney to stay with her brother Albert and his wife Frances.

'The pregnancy progressed slowly, lots of morning sickness and a very quiet life with her aunt and uncle were not what

Kitty had hoped for at this time of life. To make matters worse, she had written to Bill every week and there had been no replies. Initially she figured he was on a ship or in battle and unable to write or post anything but after a couple of months she heard through her Mum that the Butler boys had sent news to their family that they were well and having a fine old time. She assumed Bill had second thoughts once he left.

'Kitty told me she had had some thoughts of keeping the baby but once it was clear that Bill didn't love her after all she gave up all such notions. She hadn't told Bill about the baby yet in her letters, so no harm done. Frances and Albert also hinted that perhaps they could adopt the baby but having made her decision Kitty thought that a clean break would be best. The baby would be taken to its new parents soon after it was born. She probably wouldn't even see it after the birth. It made her sad but she felt she had come to terms with this as the best thing for everyone, especially the little one.'

'Oh that's so tragic', Stella said. 'Imagine, a teenager herself, having to make so many decisions and far from your parents because you are with extended family in the city. The city itself must have been a shock after living out west of Bourke.'

'Hmmm, well there was more misfortune unfortunately. Kitty carried the baby to term and everything seemed to be going well. Her doctors said she was doing well and the second half of the pregnancy had been easier than the early months. She and her aunt had become close as well and Kitty felt she had a confidante she could trust. There were even some outings to the pictures and drives to the beach. As planned, Ellen came to Sydney so that she would be there for the birth to support her daughter.

'Kitty went into labour and Uncle Albert drove her to St Margaret's Hospital. It had been agreed that Frances would stay with her for the birth if she was allowed or at least wait outside the labour ward. The labour was long and the baby was in the breach position, after 24 hours Frances had to go home to sleep. Kitty was exhausted and in terrible pain but the doctors assured her it wouldn't be much longer. I was born about five in the morning and the doctors and nurses were fussing around so much Kitty started to worry.'

'They say I almost died. I was in hospital for weeks and somewhere during that time, plans changed and Ellen decided that she would raise me as her child. So it was agreed and slowly I got strong enough to go home and from then on I was Ellen's daughter although Kitty breast fed me at the beginning.'

'So sad. I know she could still care for you, be close, but she couldn't be a proper mother,' Stella said.

'Years later, Kitty told me they were the worst days of her life. Bill didn't love her, her baby was now her sister. She couldn't sleep, she didn't want to eat. These days we would call it post-natal depression back then she was told to snap out of it'.

'I can imagine Grandma would have been saying she needed to put it behind her, that was her way', Stella said. 'These days she would have had support to help her process all those thoughts and feelings. There would be counsellors and social workers to help'.

'After she and Ellen came home to Bourke it was expected that everything would go back to normal. Kitty sent a final letter to Bill about that time, telling him everything about the baby as a kind of therapy. She assured him he was free and that she had no intentions of being a problem for him when he returned.'

'Kitty knew that Bill never received that letter because it was returned to sender. She later learnt that he had died some months before. Kitty said it felt like two years of her life had been obliterated and that a new person came out on the other side. The new Kitty was more contained, more conservative, more careful to show affection. The new Kitty cut herself off from me for a long time. Self preservation.'

'But Bill did write to Kitty. This letter is from him, isn't it?', Stella did not understand.

'That was the awful thing. The letter from Bill came after Kitty left for Sydney and Mum and Dad agreed that it should not be sent on to her. They thought it would be easier for her if she didn't have to tell Bill about the baby. Besides, they were both so young it was unlikely they would still want to get married at the end of the war. One of them would have met someone else by then surely'.

After hesitating for a minute, Eleanor added, 'And the other thing was that Bill was half Aborigine. He was fair but his mother was an Aboriginal woman from Engonnia. I hate to admit it but Mum and Dad couldn't accept that.'

'Did Kitty ever find out about the letter', Stella asked thinking this was all very Tess-of-the-D'Urbervilles-ish.

'Yes, Ellen told Kitty about the letter years later. You probably never realized but Kitty was never truly well after. She had several breakdowns and had to go to the mental hospital after her second girl, May was born. It was kept very quiet but she died of an overdose. Not the first time she had tried but that last time, Norm had gone away for a couple of days. Lillian found her when she called around for coffee one morning.

'We were all devastated of course and Mum was beside herself with guilt as well as grief. But you know the only oblique reference she made of all that history was to say she was glad that Dad hadn't lived to see his oldest daughter's final suffering.'

Eleanor took a deep drink of wine and Stella absorbed the unexpected twists. She had been ready to hear about the high drama of a child born out of wedlock and secretly raised as a sister but the depths of tragedy and suffering were cruelly unexpected.

'How did my Mum come to have these letters and photos do you think?' Stella asked.

'I assume they were in Ellen's things when Lillian cleaned out the house. She and Charlie did most of that. They probably decided to put the papers in a safe place until they decided whether to give them to Norm or to Kitty's girls. Maybe it was easiest just to leave them there. Nothing to be gained by stirring up past pain.'

'I gather from Mum's diary that Kitty married Norm a year or so after she came back from Sydney. I'm surprised after hearing all of this', Stella said, imagining how hard it must have been to pretend everything was alright and get on with her life.

'I suspect it was more about getting away from Mum and Dad, to be honest. They could be pretty controlling and Kitty had had a taste of being away from home even if it was in difficult circumstances. She'd known Norm all her life and after the whirlwind of Bill perhaps she was happy with the safe and knowable alternative', Eleanor surmised.

A while later Stella stood under the shower washing off the travel weariness and preoccupied with Kitty's story. She had packed so much emotion and turmoil into her early years that it was little wonder her resilience had run its course too early. And the goatherd? Eleanor hadn't said.

Chapter 14

Christmas dawned hot and bright, the air was drier out here than in the city. It had been a late night as Stella and Eleanor had sat up eating mince pies after the Christmas service. Eleanor was on a roll and continued to tell family stories, some of which Stella knew well but others dated to well after Lillian had left home. It seemed that Ellen and Ted had not always had a happy marriage especially when he spent more than the usual amount of time at home as became necessary in his later years when he was no longer working. Eleanor recalled lots of arguments and stormy silences during her teen years after the family had moved from Nyngan, back to Bourke for a while, before settling in Belgravia where Eleanor still lived.

After hearing so many family dramas, Stella had anticipated a poor night's sleep but she had slept deeply and was surprised to realise it was already nine o'clock as she walked into the kitchen. No sign of Eleanor yet although Stella could hear the shower running. A quick coffee she decided was what she needed before launching into the day in earnest. She was not used to having lots of family around and in a couple of hours she would be in its midst.

By midday, thirty relatives, four generations, all talking at once welcomed her to her first big Christmas since childhood. They were certainly a prolific lot on this side of the family. She, Lillian and David had been the opposite – a tight unit, self-contained. Eleanor's brood were a sprawling amalgam of talents, ages, interests and life experience. They were noisy, warm, opinionated and entirely inclusive so Stella need not have worried about feeling out of place. The chaos was undemanding if not exactly relaxing. Little was required of her in the hubbub of competing voices and special treats that kept everyone absorbed and distracted.

After lunch there was the obligatory lull when half the party adjourned to the backyard for the annual cricket match, a few others slept and one or two suggested a walk to burn off some of the calories. Stella found herself walking beside her cousin Liz who was five years younger and had lived in the same town her whole life. She had a good job as the practice manager for the local GP and her husband, who she had known since school, worked at the bank. Her youngest daughter had stayed close to home but the eldest one was currently working in New York City as a human rights lawyer. Liz was clearly proud of her but also bemused by why she wanted to live so far away.

'The work must be very rewarding', Stella said. 'Being able to help vulnerable people who have been disadvantaged by systems and corruption is remarkable. And New York is such an amazing city, so lively, always something to do.'

'Yes, of course, we are all very proud of her. She decided this year to spend the holiday season, as she calls it now, in Mexico travelling around rather than back here. I was disappointed but I did not say so. We will call her later this evening when she starts her Christmas day.'

'Are you planning a visit?' Stella asked.

Liz shook her head. 'It is such a long flight and I don't like big cities. I find Sydney completely overwhelming so I can't imagine enjoying anywhere that is even busier and dirtier, as New York is by all accounts.'

'Well that's true but aren't you curious to see where she lives and what her life is like there. One of my friends used to say that whenever I moved house she liked to see my new place so that when we chatted on the phone she could imagine where I was sitting. That was in the old days when we had landlines but the principle still applies', her voice trailed off as she realized that Liz was only half listening.

Liz took the chance to change the subject to her new grandchild. Such a delight to spend time with her and her daughter had turned out to be fantastic mother. She said that she felt blest to be able to spend so much time with them and to see the little one growing up so fast. The conversation carried on along similar lines as they made their way home. It was hot in the afternoon sun and even though they sought out the shade both cousins were hot and tired when they arrived back. Liz's husband was in the kitchen doling out cold drinks to the cricketers and the returning walkers were also grateful for his foresight.

The eating and drinking seemed to be primed to commence again around six o'clock and Stella was relieved to overhear Eleanor telling her daughter that she would like to go home soon. There were offers to run Eleanor home now and for Stella to stay longer so that she could enjoy more family time but Stella rushed to reassure that she was also happy to return with Eleanor earlier than originally planned. After loading the car with an assortment of leftovers, Anthony shuffled his mother into the car for the return drive and Stella felt herself relaxing as she made her goodbyes to the rest of the clan.

'Ah, what a lovely day', Eleanor said as she eased down into an armchair and put her feet up. They tire me out but I love it you know, keeps me going. Isn't that baby girl adorable? She will be walking before we know it'.

Stella nodded as she went to make them a cup of tea. Perhaps they would feel like some supper in a while but for now a restorative and some quiet time were called for. In fact, Eleanor was already asleep in her chair by the time Stella returned with the tea which she gently sat beside her, careful not to disturb the soft snore of her breathing. Stella smiled and went in search of her book and her headphones – some gentle moments to come back to herself after a day exposed to the largest branches of her family tree.

An hour or so later as Eleanor stirred, Stella began to busy herself making them a turkey sandwich with the leftovers. A glass of wine for her and a refreshed cup of tea for Eleanor were all they needed to accompany their simple meal after a day of rich indulgences. Eleanor was clearly exhausted and so they both enjoyed an early night as the light outside and the worst of the summer heat faded.

Next morning the cicadas began their singing early. Stella stretched fully awake, the tendrils of a dream eluding her. She was feeling refreshed after a satisfyingly sound sleep, having escaped the indigestion that she had feared after all that eating yesterday. Eleanor would not be up for another couple of hours and Stella decided to walk around the town for some exercise and to enjoy the country air.

Her grandparents had moved here soon Lillian's wedding and for Eleanor it seemed this was where many of her best memories were formed. Unlike Lillian, for whom the property outside Bourke and the pub near Nyngan were the places of childhood and youth, Eleanor had mostly known the life of a small country town. She had been about twelve years old when they moved and she had formed lifelong friendships. Now her own family kept her tied to this place. In fact, Ellen's mother's family had come from near here before she married and moved to Bourke. Lillian had once said that Ma, her grandmother, was one of the strongest people she knew but that she had missed her parents and living in this milder more abundant landscape. It seems she had written to her own mother every week, right up until the time of old Granny's death.

The walk around the central part of town did not take long although there were newly developed areas on the higher land to the north and also along the main highway. Stella counted three pubs in two blocks of what was the main street. There was an old bakery, a post office, supermarket, pharmacy and the ubiquitous stock and station agent. One bank remained and the other buildings that looked like they had been banks in better days had been turned into cafes or craft shops. No one else was around at this early hour and walking up the hill, Stella came to the small stone school buildings where Eleanor had completed the schooling she started near Nyngan. There were playing fields and netball courts beside the school buildings. Stella recalled that Eleanor had been a talented netball player and she had played for the district or possibly even the state. No doubt some of today's rheumatic joints could be traced back to those days.

The clock on the post office struck nine o'clock as Stella arrived back at her aunt's ready for a coffee and breakfast. They had a date for a drive around the district that morning before

Stella headed back to the city after lunch but she was still surprised to see Eleanor up, dressed and with breakfast laid out ready for her.

'It is a beautiful morning. Have you been out for a walk?' she asked before going on without waiting for a reply. 'Have some breakfast and when you are ready we can go for a drive while its still not too hot'.

And so half an hour later they were settled in Stella's car and Eleanor was giving directions to drive west along the highway. After ten minutes they turned onto a smaller road and from there onto a dirt lane. Curious, Stella waited for Eleanor to reveal their destination knowing she was loving the suspense.

'You can stop here', she finally said. 'This is my great grandmother's old home. Ma grew up here and when we first came back down this way, Mum and I would visit while Granny was still alive. I only remember a very old woman who did not talk much, sitting in the kitchen. She was always dressed in black and the house was always dark inside. She would have been in her nineties then, she was ninety five when she died, a grand age!'

'Wow, I don't even remember Lillian talking about her to be honest.', Stella said.

'Well she did not know her really. They may have met once but that would be all. Mum used to tell me stories about her when we were coming here. They were stories that Ma had told her I suppose.'

The house in front of them was white timber with a verandah at the front and enormous garden all around, now in disrepair. There were trees in the next paddock, possibly an orchard and two small sheds. The most striking feature, besides the buttressed sides of the verandah, was the stately circular drive that led to a portico through which the house could be entered. Stella half expected a horse and carriage to drive up and deliver its passengers. It was a large house, clearly her great-great-grandparents had been well off. Not in the same league as some of the big pastoralists" homesteads around the district but still a solid statement of social status.

'Mum said that in her day, Granny was a firebrand but she also had all the expected accomplishments of a well brought up young woman, able to oversee her own household and family, embroider, play the piano. She was also a writer - poetry that was published in the local newspaper and once she had one of her poems published in a literary magazine. Not happy with simply writing, she started her own newspaper which was very successful and which she eventually sold when her husband died in the 1930s. He died 30 years before her and she continued to run the property after he passed away.'

'A strong woman', Stella observed, thinking that there was still a good deal she didn't know about that reef in the family. And hadn't Lillian said that her mother also wrote poetry, an artistic lot as well.

'After Granny died, I lived in this house with Mum and Dad for a few years. Lillian came to visit once or twice a year. That was before you were born.'

It was approaching midday as Stella and Eleanor drove back for a quick lunch and Stella readied her things for her return.

'I will visit you again when I go on my drive out west', Stella said. 'I want to wait until the weather is cooler, so around March or April I expect'.

'I would like that', Eleanor said. 'Come before your trip and I will have whatever photos I can find of the old places for you'.

Making her promises and saying her goodbyes, Stella started the long drive back to the city. She was pleased it would take a while as she felt that re-establishing her usual headspace could take a while as well.

Chapter 15

After the short break for Christmas, Stella was pleased to be going back to work. Some time at the beach and catching up on household chores left her feeling relaxed and ready for a new year. She'd enjoyed having time to read all the books she had accumulated for a binge over summer but noticed that the days dragged out in the afternoons if she had not made plans. There had even been afternoon naps on a few days - most unlike her.

The only work task that she had succumbed to was spending a few afternoons contacting colleagues in Europe to search out a new PhD supervisor for Laura. Finally a friend based at Imperial College London had come back with two suggestions, one in Hamburg and the other in Cologne. Stella contacted both and without revealing any details explained that she had an excellent student looking for a place in Germany. She was delighted when both came back positively and she made the necessary introductions to Laura via email. She decided to offer to set up a Skype meeting with them, Laura and herself to discuss each prospect in more detail. It was not much but she hoped it would help Laura make the best possible move.

Some days later when Stella dropped by St Gertrude's she found Pete was out. She assumed he was visiting with his nephew and was pleased he was making that connection with family. She knew he missed his little dog so hopefully they were both making the most of a visit.

Her only other social outing was to see Anna and as she drove there she reflected that her circle had contracted in recent years as more of her friends were in relationships or turned towards family. A mix of ageing parents and kids who were beginning to have their own families filled their days. No so for her. She brushed the thought away, not ready, not wanting to follow where that led.

Anna had spent the holidays preparing the family home for sale. The painters were still finishing the upstairs bedrooms and the gardener was literally walking out the front gate as Stella arrived.

'The house is looking great', Stella said, knowing that Anna and Rex were hoping to put it on the market at the end of January.

'Thanks, yes, makes me wish I had done this decluttering years ago so that I could enjoy the space while I am living here. The hardest thing was convincing the girls to take all their old stuff. There were books, toys, puzzles, even school trophies in boxes under the bed. Against huge resistance I finally managed to get them to sort through and take whatever they wanted'.

Stella remembered having recently done the same at her parents old house and voiced some sympathy for the magnitude of the task and the emotional pull the girls would be experiencing. Anna, back to her most practical self, discounted these finer feelings with a sweep of her hand. No doubt she too had had to move past the sentimental.

'And how was Christmas?' Stella changed the subject.

'You know I was worried it would be awful but in the end it was really delightful', Anna was smiling and packing a box as she spoke.

'Claire and Jane came Christmas Eve as you know and stayed overnight. We watched the carols on tele before taking a walk to look at all the decorated yards a few streets away. Then of course, much eating and drinking on Christmas day'.

You had already started cooking when I was here the day before so I assume it was quite the feast for lunch'.

Yes of course, way too much food—seafood, turkey with all the trimmings, pavlova. It was never-ending. Claire has been doing a wine appreciation course so she picked matching wines which were delicious but had me asleep on the couch mid-afternoon'.

Did the family stay a few days? 'Stella asked.

Anna shook her head, 'They left here early evening, piled with leftovers, to go to other events and I had been invited to the neighbours' for a light dinner so I headed over there. What about you, how was seeing the big family?'

'It was good', Stella said but Anna could hear the hesitation in her voice.

'But?'

'No really it was good. I had a great gossip with Aunty Eleanor about all the family stories and learnt about a few skeletons along the way. Nothing sensational mind you,' she said realising that she did not want to get into Kitty's story just then.

'Christmas day was really full on with all the cousins and their kids. Everyone was lovely and the whole day was a great festive occasion. But you know me, I need my own space and I was grateful for a quiet night afterwards'.

'Boxing Day we drove out to the house my great grandmother was born in and that was interesting. I had not realized that she'd come from that area so more family history to discover. Aunty Eleanor was enjoying the audience and she is great company. I will call in again when I drive out to Bourke. I think I told you I'm planning a pilgrimage when the weather cools down.'

'Can I ask you a favour?', Anna asked, changing the subject. 'Would you come with me to look at apartments once we put this place on the market'.

'Of course', Stella nodded. 'You know I love looking at real estate. What area are you thinking?'

'Not too far from here. It's close to the kids and work and I have friends from when the girls were at school. I don't really want to have to find my way around a new community.'

'Sounds sensible', Stella agreed. The conversation turned to the real estate market and what Anna could reasonably afford. What could be compromised and what were must-haves? Stella reflected later that it was the typical Sydney conversation of the newly divorced middle-aged woman.

Wednesday morning Stella was at Mandalay Cottage early, ready to finally start her research in earnest after the holiday break. There were no signs of anything having changed while she was away. The usual suspects were sitting smoking outside, the patient queue for showers was out the door, a few people sat in the cafe but it was quieter than normal.

Alice, the volunteer coordinator, smiled hello and welcomed her back while at the same time negotiating with a client who thought he ought to be at the head of the shower queue although he had just arrived. Stella was pleased to see that one of the people in the café was Jenny. No doubt she was waiting for Teresa or Lucy to join her. They had become a good support network for each other, different as they were. They generally tried to stay at the same hostel but that was often impossible given the high demand for refuge services and the limited spaces.

'Hi Jen', Stella began. 'Do you mind if I join you?'

Jenny nodded and pointed to the chair opposite. 'How was your break?' she asked. 'I've forgotten, were you going away somewhere'.

'It was good. Yes, I went to the country for a couple of days to stay with my aunt. Christmas day was with all her kids and grandkids. A real clan. More people than I would normally choose to be honest but they were all lovely. What about you? Were you here?'

'Yes, they put on a good spread and all the regulars and staff were here. I'm not a big fan of Christmas but this year was ok, you know. One of the only good things about getting older is that I'm learning to be realistic in my expectations and that takes off a heap of pressure.'

'Where are you staying at the moment?' Stella asked.

'Ah, did you hear? That was the best Christmas present ever. I have finally got a place in public housing. I can hardly believe it but I'm in a little flat in Waterloo. It's old and smells like an old man's feet but I couldn't be happier.'

'Fantastic! Well that is cause for celebration. When did you move in?'

'Just two days ago. Lucy and Tez came to help me clean it before I moved. My god, you should have seen the toilet, it was filthy and the bath was so black I thought the enamel had lifted. But we scrubbed it and it's almost white again. The staff here helped me get some basics, you know, a bed, table and fridge.'

'It must be so good to have your own space. Not having to pack up all your stuff every few days or hide things so they aren't stolen'.

'I feel like I can relax at last. The past few months in refuges has been especially tough but before that wasn't great either. Every day I would worry there was going to be a fight. It was like walking on eggshells. Sometimes I would find myself walking around the block or sitting in the park to avoid going home'.

Stella let the silence sit comfortably between them while Jenny drank her coffee. Her cup had brown circles that looked like they could have been used for carbon dating - must be stone cold. Eventually Jenny looked up and offered to be the first interviewee for Stella's research.

'Really, would you be comfortable doing that', Stella wanted to give Jenny a hug and at the same time she knew she needed to give her space to reconsider her decision, to not feel obliged. She should have known, even from their relatively brief acquaintance, that Jenny was the sort of woman who having made up her mind would carry through.

'Yes, absolutely sure. Give me a day or so to think about what I want to say and bring your tape-recorder with you on Friday'.

'I will just use the phone of that's ok with you', Stella said, 'And thank you so much. It will be an enormous honour to hear your story. Thank you for trusting me to listen. Shall we meet here on Friday morning or would you rather we go somewhere else?'

'No, here is good. Maybe you can shout me a real coffee so I don't have to drink this shit', Jenny laughed.

'You're on', Stella agreed. 'It is the least I can do'.

The rest of the shift passed uneventfully and Stella was already planning how she should approach Friday and what she still needed to do in the meantime so that she was ready to use the information most efficiently as she started to gather it. She needed to do a good job of this or word would spread and finding other participants would be difficult. A day at the office tomorrow would let her rehearse and review the literature which she had not looked at for a few weeks.

Friday morning was hot and the air was sticky with the promise of storms in the afternoon. Sultry could be deliciously indolent but this morning it was claustrophobic, not to mention anti-social, Stella thought as she noticed damp circles already starting to appear on her T-shirt.

Public transport would not to be pretty but parking was impossible near Mandalay Cottage. A lot of people took January off, so Stella hoped the train would not be too packed and she would not find herself standing nose to arm-pit with fellow commuters. Being on the short side had some real disadvantages in this weather. Fortunately luck was on her side and the air conditioning in the train even seemed to be working properly.

After buying two coffees from the hole-in-the-wall café around the corner from Mandalay, Stella was pleased to see Jenny sitting in the shade at the entrance waiting for her. They had the bench to themselves and agreed it would be more comfortable than moving inside at least while the breeze persisted.

People say that only men talk shoulder to shoulder but given the personal nature of this conversation it seemed an appropriate way to start off. Jenny needed no urging to talk about her experiences and what had led her to a period of homelessness. Of course, she knew what Stella was trying to achieve having given her feedback on her interview approach a few weeks before. The tremor in her voice sounded more like urgency than trepidation. Her story had been boarded up for too long, it needed to see the light of day.

'Jim and I got together ten years ago in my mid-thirties. I was divorced and working as a bookkeeper for a family business. Jim was a friend of one of the other guys at work and sometimes he would join us for Friday drinks at the local pub.

'One thing led to another and we started to go out and before long he had moved into my place. Back then I had a nice two bedroom apartment that I had bought after the divorce settlement. I still had a mortgage but I was pleased to be independent and felt like I was working towards security longer term.

'Making sure I had a nest egg and a back up plan if I suddenly lost my job had been the safety net I'd had in place ever since I started working and left home. My parents were working class, country folk. Salt of the earth but not in a position to help me if I ever ran into trouble. And so I had made it a habit to live within my means and put a bit aside for a rainy day. My ex-husband, Bruce was also very thrifty and we managed to buy a little house soon after our wedding.

'I was married for five years but it was a disaster from the get-go. Bruce was kind and considerate when we were going out and I was drawn to his steadfastness. Besides he was besotted with me, the ultimate aphrodisiac. Once we were married, his steadfastness seemed more like lack of ambition and his kindness came to be a timidity and meekness that drove me crazy. His best traits brought out the worst in me. I would set psychological traps to befuddle and catch him out. I would subject him to silences as I fumed and he fussed about in a bewildered stupor trying to work out what he had done wrong. I am not proud of my behaviour and my youth was no excuse for the suffering I inflicted on him. I was heartless.

'The divorce was quick and painless, at least for me. We sold the house and I used the money for a deposit on the apartment. I only saw Bruce once after that. A few years later when I was in the city, I ran into him at the train station and he was married with a baby daughter. He seemed to be very happy.

'So by the time I met Jim, I was reasonably comfortable. You don't get rich on a bookkeeper's salary but I was doing alright. I had even managed a couple of overseas holidays with a girlfriend. First time we had gone to Thailand and then the next year to Bali. They were good times.

'In the beginning, Jim was great. He cooked and cleaned, he bought me flowers every week, we went out with his friends and mine and I was loving the companionship not to mention the sex. Sometimes on the weekend, he would have a beer or two too many but his job was stressful and it seemed fair enough that he let off steam.

'After a few months, I noticed that he would occasionally say something cutting, contempt in his voice, putting me down. I called him out and he apologized straight away each time.'

Jenny's breathing was audible, like she was walking up steep hill. After a few moments, Stella asked, 'When you say he would say something cutting what sort of things?'

Jenny still seemed to be catching her breath, 'There was one time, silly example really. We were driving to a party at a friend's new house. Neither of us had been there before and I drove past the house twice without realizing. On the second time around he said in this really harsh voice, 'For fuck's sake you stupid cow can't you get anything right!' or something like that. It was the disdain as much as the words. You know that expression, if looks could kill – well that was the quality in his voice.'

'Jim's Dad had been in the army and when Jim talked about his childhood it sounded like a military operation. Everything was planned and shipshape, there was not too much room for dreaming and playing by all accounts. He was very proud of his Dad but also felt that he had been a disappointment himself. Never quite fast enough on the track or smart enough in school. Those feelings of being less than he should have been stayed with him as an adult.

'I'm not making excuses for him but over the years I learnt to understand him. We had been together three or four years when Jim was made redundant. He was in his late forties by then and it was hard for him to find another job. He must have gone to 20 interviews but no one was prepared to give him a chance. The longer he was out of work the harder it became to even get an interview.

'He started drinking more and when he drank he became angry and argumentative, looking for a fight over the smallest thing. He would see a put down in every thing I said. I couldn't win so I found myself placating him, avoiding anything contentious, stroking his ego at every opportunity.

'At first that helped but it was one Christmas when things became really bad. We had been to a friend's place for lunch and someone had asked me. 'How's the house-husband?' I tried to deflect the comment but I could see that Jim had overheard and storm clouds were brewing. I made a couple of banal comments about the lunch party on the drive home but Jim wouldn't be drawn.

'That evening was the first time he hit me. He accused me of flirting with one of the other men at lunch and when I laughed because I thought it was a joke he slapped my face and hit the side of my head.

'I was stunned. I had never encountered physical violence and I had never suspected that Jim was capable of it. I slept in the spare room that night and by morning all had been smoothed over and it seemed like a bad dream.

'A few weeks after that Jim was talking with a friend who convinced him to invest in a new business. He would be a thirty percent partner in the business and the business plan predicted healthy profits in both the short and long term. His friend would own fifty percent of the business as he had invented this device that they were planning to commercialise and the friend's accountant would be the third investor. Jim wanted us to remortgage the apartment, although it was technically mine, as a way to raise the capital for the investment. It had only taken one conversation with a bank to realise that there was no way he would be able to get a loan while he was unemployed.

'Initially, I refused but eventually he worked me around and I agreed – against my better judgement. For six months he was on a high. He had purpose and prospects again. He was busy helping with the new business and he was optimistic. Life was good and I was happy I had agreed to help him raise the capital for the project.

'The new company had a small board of directors as well as the owners and just before the second year annual financials were being sorted there was some sort of disagreement among them. Jim's friend, the inventor accused the chairman and accountant of diverting funds from production to shore up sub-contracts which were held by their companies. Jim was caught in the middle and became very stressed. I noticed that he had started drinking more again and things got worse as overseas competitors took a chunk of business off them. They suddenly had too much product and not enough buyers and the creditors were demanding payment. The beatings started again and this time they were more frequent and more violent.

'The company was unravelling and I started to worry that our investment was at risk. Jim wasn't the only one drinking too much and we had a lot of fights, loud angry arguments as I accused him of putting me in a financially vulnerable situation.

'Looking back I would say what was happening in the board room and the company was even worse. They were self-destructing and making bad business decisions. They finally declared bankruptcy but not before the debts were entirely out of hand.

'We lost everything; my apartment included. Jim became more and more resentful as I found us rental accommodation and continued to work to pay the bills. The violence went up another notch - it was unrelenting. I would lock myself in the bedroom some nights in fear of my life. He had threatened to kill me several times and I believed he would do it if I didn't get out of there.

'So I left but he found me at my new place and threatened me again. It was a nightmare and I could see no way out. My friends and family had no real idea about what was happening and my boss was losing patience with the number of sick days I was taking.

'The week before my fiftieth birthday, things came to a head. Jim was waiting outside my flat when I got home from work. He was drunk and maybe high on something as well. He had a gun and he was waving it about as he shouted that I had ruined his life, taken everything he cared about. Ironic in theory but terrifying in reality. He hit me around the head with the gun, punched my face and head butted me, I think. I was unconscious for a while on the front steps. I eventually dragged myself inside and called an ambulance. No one seemed to have seen what happened or if they did, they did not want to get involved. Who could blame them?

'When I called work two days later the boss told me not to bother coming back. He gave me two weeks pay and there I was. I started living in my car as the rent became impossible and I would shower in a park or hostel. I tried to go for job interviews for a couple of weeks but it was hopeless and degrading. I looked like shit, I was drinking too much and not sleeping or eating properly. No employer in their right mind was going to touch me.

'So one thing led to another and I ended up here, talking to you'.

'God, Jenny what an awful story. I had no idea what you have been through. Do you still worry Jim will find you again? He doesn't sound exactly stable,' Stella finally said.

'I used to worry because I can assure you he was truly scary when he was in a rage but he died a year ago. He was hit by a car walking across the road late at night near central. The driver did not see him and he walked straight out in front of the car. I had to identify the body, still officially next of kin.'

Stella opened her mouth but what did she have to offer, a platitude at best. There were no words, she thought, worthy of the pain and terror Jenny had known.

Jenny seemed to read her mind. 'The social workers and domestic violence groups call it lived experience, well I have shit loads of lived experience', Jenny said with a hard snort that may have been a laugh.

'Did you ever feel that things could have gone differently?', Stella started to ask.

'I think every day about what I could have done to change things. I should have thrown Jim out the first time he slapped me. That's the easy answer but there are not easy answers. Have you seen that movie Sliding Doors? My life was the horror movie version or at least that's what I tell the counsellor'.

'Are you still seeing a counsellor?', Stella was surprised although she was not sure why.

'Sure, I see the psychologist here. She's ok and maybe it has helped. I don't blame myself anymore but I still haven't forgiven Jim. It's a poison I carry around and it kills a lot of the pain but it kills indiscriminately. It's toxic and it will poison the rest of my life unless I stop hating him.'

The two women sat for a while. Stella was the one who needed to get her breath back now. Jenny had run the marathon but Stella was the one with the searing stitch in her side and heart pushing against her sternum. How did someone experience all that anguish, loss, vulnerability and not become a total victim? Stella doubted she would have the courage to claw her way back the way that Jenny was doing.

'Don't look so sad', Jenny said. 'You know my story is pretty tame compared to most around here. I had a good childhood; I had an education and have mostly worked. Even my relationships have been more good than bad. Being in public housing and on the pension wasn't in any of my plans but plenty of people have it worse. You had better prepare yourself if you are going to keep on with these interviews'.

'Hmm, you know when you said your life is a version of sliding doors?', Stella was following a random thought that had come into her head. 'What would have happened if you had talked to someone, a psychologist, a friend, whatever, before you lent Jim all that money or even after you finally left him?'

'Who knows, maybe it would have been the same, maybe worse. I can't go back to change it and I wouldn't be me if it hadn't happened. You know Stella, life isn't a script, there is no eraser and consequences won't be cheated', Jenny smiled self-consciously at her home grown philosophy.

She went on, 'But I can tell you, what's helped me most has been practical stuff. Sometimes cash, a bed in a hostel, the loan of a phone to call ahead for accommodation, a hot shower, clean clothes can make all the difference to your day. You can't work your way back if there are no gaps in the wall, if ladders aren't occasionally held steady. Without a safe base you can never dare to live again'.

'When you say that, you remind me of something from when I was a kid', Stella said. 'It's a silly, little event from school but it has stayed with me for some reason. I was in religion class when I was about seven or eight. There were probably only ten of us, it was a small school, and Sister Edna Agatha been telling us about how fortunate we were compared to children in poor countries. She asked us all to tell her one thing that we should thank god for. Most of the kids said things like toys, their Mum and Dad, a dog, their favourite doll but I said my bed. For some reason Sister Agatha thought this was hilarious and I was totally embarrassed. I didn't understand what was so funny. For me, my bed meant safety and warmth and my answer seemed perfectly reasonable.'

'Sister Agatha must have been a cow and in her line of work homelessness wasn't a prospect'.

They talked for a while longer but Jenny was shifting in her seat and Stella pushed her chair back, also ready to finish up. Time to clear the head and untangle the spirit. Stella felt the weight of the privilege Jenny had given her but right now she craved solitude. She knew she would not try to look at the transcript for this interview in the coming week or two.

Chapter 16

Jenny must have given her a good review because in the following week, several women agreed to be interviewed by Stella. Lucy and Teresa who had previewed the original questions with Jenny were not among them, however. Perhaps the bungled first draft of the interview structure had scared them off. Stella hoped not but she did appreciate the tapestry of experiences that were shared with her.

Between interviews, Stella spent many hours with Anna looking for a new apartment. The initial property inspections covered a diverse mix of places, in size, aspect, even suburb. From her own experience, Stella knew that Anna was really using these inspections to become clearer in her own mind about what she really wanted but Anna was less aware that that was what she was doing and after two weeks she was becoming frustrated. The following weeks however were more focused and they started looking at apartments that were genuine possibilities and within the budget. There were even a couple of unsuccessful offers submitted. Stella sensed that Anna was starting to close in on her new home and she had promised to give her all the following weekend. There was only one caveat, she really needed to take an hour or two to see Pete as she had missed her regular catch ups with him.

In the information that Stella had provided to her interviewees, she had indicated that their identity would be entirely protected. No name, date of birth, address or other identifiers. She had decided to give each woman a pseudonym that she and they would agree on at the beginning of the interview. In this way they could see their contribution to her work if they ever cared to look but only the two of them could decode the interviewees identity.

Marcia chose her name for Marcia Brady, a favourite television show from her teens. True they had blonde hair in common but all resemblance stopped there. This Marcia was so thin she could break under the pressure of her own stoop. She told Stella that she had been a cellist and when she finished her degree in the early eighties, she was offered a scholarship to a music school in the USA. She had graduated top of her class in Sydney but even so when she was accepted at Berkeley everyone was amazed.

'I had lived at home until then, not even been overseas for a holiday. I had no idea what to expect in California but I was desperate to go as soon as I could', Marcia said. 'A lot of the students were politically active especially about AIDS and homosexuality. Even some of the professors were flamboyantly gay. It was much more open there than it had been back in Sydney'.

'Were you part of that scene', Stella asked.

'I experimented a bit, even had a girlfriend for a while. Ash was this gorgeous redhead who was studying composition. She's semi-famous these days.

'But I experimented more with drugs. Everyone was trying something and it seemed so sophisticated and exciting after boring old Sydney'.

She recalled her first weeks there - finding accommodation in a share house with fellow musicians, making new friends and finding her way around the city. There were late nights, a good amount of alcohol and the underground club scene.

'The club scene was just the best, intoxicating. I couldn't get enough of it'.

How were your studies going with all of that partying,' Stella asked with a small laugh in her voice to dispel any suggestion that she was judging.

'My grades were great. I loved my teachers and I was learning a lot. We had well known musicians and conductors come to work with us. Everything was going so well'.

Stella waited for Marcia to go on.

'About the time I broke up with Ash I started using acid. She didn't like it especially when I had a couple of bad trips that scared her. It was one of the reasons we broke up.

'I don't remember the first full-on psychotic episode, just the terror of waking up in a psych hospital. My parents who had flown to the States were arguing with each other beside my bed. The doctors convinced them that I needed ECT and I must have gone along with it. If anyone asked me'.

She made an odd grimace, 'The genie was out of its box and years of being zapped and dosed up with pills have just made it hard to think straight. My memory is shot and I get confused when I'm somewhere new'.

'How to you manage day to day?' Stella asked, realizing how vulnerable Marcia must be when she is sleeping rough.

'It's not always pretty but anything is better than being in a psych unit. Most of the time I live in boarding houses but the last one closed down and the case worker here is helping me find a new one'.

Stella found it hard to reconcile the small, blonde woman with her quiet voice and gentle manner with the story she was telling. It was true her tone was flat, and her fingers constantly fiddled but you would probably overlook that if it was not for a skittishness in her eyes. Stella asked if she still played music.

'Can't bear it, pierces my head like a dentist's drill.

'Look sorry I have to go now', she said, getting up quickly and making her way over to a group of regulars who were laughing and smoking. Maybe I pushed that too far Stella thought but goodness what a story.

And then there was Amal who had come from Sri Lanka for an arranged marriage. She had followed the traditional path of entering her mother-in-law's household and had been bullied by the other women. Her husband had beat her and eventually he divorced her when she did not produce any children. She was literally thrown out onto the streets with no family or friends, no money and no rights. A Muslim women's group were providing her with accommodation for a few weeks and she was desperately trying to convince her family to send money so that she could come home. Her father was ashamed of her, the whole family was angry with her. Only her sister seemed willing to listen and Amal prayed that she would help her return to Kandy.

A normal life in the suburbs was how Tanya described her former life. She worked in a bank, had two kids, a decent husband and a mortgage. She was missus average until the day she was tempted to transfer a small amount of a client's money to her own account. Success led to greater risk taking as the amounts grew until after three years she was charged with having stolen almost three quarters of a million dollars in bank fraud. She spent four years in gaol and she had been released two weeks ago. Her husband and kids had moved to Perth and did not want to see her, she had no money and no friends. An old aunt had offered her a sofa for a couple of weeks until she found a job and could rent somewhere herself. Finding a job seemed like the most impossible task. Who would want to employ her? Four years of unexplained absence from the workforce would raise suspicion. Yesterday she had been to see a woman who helped women rejoin the workforce. She had helped Tanya rewrite her CV and practice some interview questions. She had even provided her with an outfit to wear to interviews, a smart black skirt and red rayon blouse. Her aunt did not have Wi-Fi so Tanya was visiting Mandalay each morning to check her emails and prepare for interviews. Her self-worth had been decimated but there was a lightness about her of hopefulness that Stella almost envied.

The youngest woman that Stella interviewed was Diane.

'I came to Sydney to go to Uni but it's not working out. I failed my exams this semester and I am going to drop out'.

'What will you do', Stella asked, thinking one semester was hardly long enough to be sure either way.

'Honestly I have no idea. I hate living here. I don't fit in at college. It's like there is this big secret that no one is letting me into - I am always on the outside trying to figure out the right thing to say and do.

'If I drop out I'll have to find somewhere else to live. The residential college is very strict about that. Not that I want to stay there. It's a bitchy hothouse but I can't tell Mum that. She loved it there when she was at Uni. She told me all the initiation stories, what a lark it was, what great friends she made'.

'Do you think if you lived somewhere else that you might like Uni better as well', Stella didn't want to push too much but she was curious.

'Maybe, I've been feeling like I can't do anything well lately and then I don't want to study and I can't get motivated to do my assignments. I used to love school – now it is too hard. I'm not smart enough, I haven't made a single friend'.

Stella was hardly an expert but Diane sounded depressed and she knew that the staff at Mandalay would be on to it. Certainly her decision making was not sharp especially when she talked about the option of living on the streets being preferable to admitting to her parents that she was dropping out. Stella hoped she would find the courage to talk to her parents and maybe even give Uni a bit more of a go.

'What brought you to Mandalay', Stella wondered.

'Yeah, I know I'm not homeless, at least not yet. No, the woman in charge here, Rosemary, is it? Yeah, she gave this talk in O-week and one of the things she said was if you ever need someone to talk to we are always ready to listen. So here I am...'

Realising she was perilously close to offering advice, Stella asked Diane if she could pass on some of what she had said to one of the workers at Mandalay. It was not Stella's role to counsel but she was sure that with some steering in the right direction that Diane could avoid a big mistake.

Stella was touched by each story but she also had an overwhelming sense of just how ordinary these women were. Their story could be anyone's, could have been hers but fate was indiscriminate. Carly's story more than any of the others found Stella having to remind herself to stay objective in this research. Her parents were from the bush and they had met when they were both working on a property between Wellington and Dubbo.

Carly's father had been taken from his family when he was a toddler because his mother already had four children and the authorities believed she couldn't cope. He was adopted by a kind family but he carried a pain and a vulnerability that made him lash out at people who he thought were putting him down. Carly's mother left him and went to live with her own mother when Carly was old enough to start school.

Welfare workers made regular visits and the family lived in dread that Carly might be taken because her mother did not have work and she was a single parent. Eventually it became too much and Carly's mum took her and moved to the city, hoping to find both work and obscurity. She did not let anyone know where she was going, even her own mother at first, in case the authorities tried to find her.

When Carly left school, she started a TAFE course in childcare because she liked children and there were plenty of jobs. But her boyfriend at the time had other ideas. He was older than her and always had plenty of cash. He could make enough money for both of them, she didn't need to work, he told her. Everything was fine until the day the police came to arrest him for drug dealing and armed robbery. Carly knew he was into some shady stuff but had no idea how serious. The police did not believe her, her mother called her a liar. Carly said she felt like an insect, watched, likely to be squashed at any moment. Heroin had become an escape and working the streets near Mandalay a necessity.

It was late Friday afternoon as Carly said goodbye at the end of her interview and turned to say to Stella. 'I will go and see Mum. Maybe I can still get my shit together if she'll have me'.

Stella nodded and smiled a little sadly. 'We all need second chances sometimes, let her give you one'. As she walked to the train station she was still thinking about Carly and generations of trauma. Her toughness was a veneer, bravura that would chip easily.

Stella's skin prickled and her brain clanged with indecision. It felt wrong to use Carly's story, her vulnerability was so far beyond Stella's understand that she worried she could never do it justice. But not to include it, denied her a voice she had chosen to make heard.

Pulling herself back to the late afternoon sunshine, Stella knew she needed to objectify the interview, look at it academically. Another act of cowardice?

She was running early for her date at the pub with Anna but that was a good thing today as she needed to reframe and recharge. Stella walked to a table at the back of the outdoors area and pulled out her novel to read over a glass of white wine while she waited. It would be at least half an hour before Anna arrived, enough time to let her mind relax into the weekend ahead.

Stella was contemplating the merits of waiting until her friend arrived before she ordered a second glass of wine when she saw her hurrying through the pub door, damp forehead, red cheeks, a flurry of apologies for being late and complaints about the humidity. Anna, bless her, left no space for preoccupation with anything. Living in her moment was the only option and Stella let herself be drawn into its vortex.

'Would you be an angel and get me some water while I go to the ladies?', Anna asked as she unloaded two brimming bags onto the seat beside Stella and bustled off to freshen up.

'That's better', she said a few minutes later as she swallowed the cold water and fanned herself with the menu. 'I caught the bus, my first mistake, and then I had to carry these bags the three blocks down here so I'm like a wet rag'.

Stella made sympathetic noises while Anna turned to the larger of the two bags. 'I have some brochures for apartments I want us to look at tomorrow. Old school, I know, but I find it easier than looking up websites endlessly.'

'This one looks nice', Stella said pointing to an older style apartment that appeared to be well renovated.

'Maybe', Anna was less sure. 'I have been leaning more towards this newly built one. It seems so clean and fresh. I like the idea that no one has lived there before me'.

'Yes, although at least with older buildings you generally know their problem. Did you see that story that has been on the news about a new block that is structurally unsound? It would make me nervous unless I was confident in the builder', Stella said.

'That's true. Well let's see what they look like tomorrow. The inspections are at 10:30 and 11:30 so we will have plenty of time to see both. And probably these other two as well although I'm not as keen on them, at least on paper.'

'How was your week?' Anna asked, apparently content to move on to another subject.

'Good, I've made great progress with my research but the stories these women tell are so sad. I sit there in my average, boring life while they tell me about how violence, drugs, mental illness, crime and life's capricious unfairness has left them vulnerable and usually alone. I didn't expect to be able to see myself in the shoes of these women. Most of them are not so different to you and me'. Stella stopped, realizing she was releasing her bottled up distress more liberally on her friend than she had intended.

'Sorry', she apologized with a half laugh. 'Don't you hate it when people tell how their week really was when you were only trying to relax at the end of a long week'.

'No, of course I want to hear about what's been happening. It sounds full on but you have done interviews like this before haven't you. Are these worse than usual?' Anna asked.

'Not so much worse but more relatable. I've realized I must have this deep seated fear that one day I could be in their situation. I find myself noticing safe, dry options for where I could sleep if I was homeless. You know, vacant shop fronts with deep awnings, that sort of thing'.

'Well it won't ever come to that. You can always stay with me', Anna said laughing at the unlikely scenario her friend was describing.

'I know you think I'm being ridiculous but even so…'Stella let her voice fade as she shook her head and straightened her back. 'Let me buy you a drink on the strength of that. Will you have a white wine?'

'Yes definitely. Now that I've cooled down, I would love a wine and maybe some nuts or olives if they have them'.

As Stella made her way back to the table, balancing glasses and a small bowl, she saw that Anna was on her phone. Not wanting to interrupt she put everything on the table and turned to her book until the call ended.

'That was Rex. He called to tell me that he and the floozy are moving in together. He said he wanted me to hear it from him rather than the kids.'

'Are you ok with it?' Stella asked.

'I'm surprised myself but yes I am actually. It has been six months and I am feeling ready to move on. I am looking forward to having my own place and also', Anna paused and her inflection promised something unexpected. 'I am going on a date tomorrow.'

'Really, that's great', Stella said hoping she didn't sound half-hearted but also thinking it was possibly too soon. Is it someone you met online? That dating profile must have done the trick'.

'Actually, its someone you know. Steve asked me to go for dinner.'

'Steve, from my work. Wow! I would never have guessed that'.

'I know, what you are thinking. Not my type! And you may be right but I've decided that I need to live a little dangerously. I have been in the same relationship all my adult life', Anna spread her hands and Stella caught hold of them.

'Just be careful. I like Steve as a colleague but he has form when it comes to women'.

'Of course but it will be nice to go out somewhere for dinner and have a man pay attention to me. I have felt invisible for months and I miss male company. Don't worry I am not getting ahead of myself but I have to start somewhere even if it is only a practice run'.

As Stella rode in the taxi home she found herself wondering why it had been so long since she dated. Sure, Brian had been a creep but nothing bad had actually happened. There was a complacency in being single that she should stir herself out of but she wasn't sure she wanted to anymore.

Compared to Carly whose life had roller-coastered her into trouble and even Anna who should have whiplash from life's sudden change in direction, Stella's life was beige. Things happened in an orderly fashion, no enormous highs and well moderated lows. What would happen if she let herself push through that armed wall, breached the safe zone?

Even her mother had had adventures that made her own life seem tame. Stella reached for Lillian's diary which she had not looked at since near Christmas time and turned to one of the last entries - from the time when Lillian had decided to leave home and take a job in Sydney. Stella had never heard her mother talk about why she left home although she often recalled her years working in the city with fondness. Lillian could hardly be described as a risk taker; she was the consummate wife and mother but sometimes Stella had caught a glimpse of the young woman she must have been. Funny how our parents are permanently middle aged, at least until they go beyond that, to become old.

December 1954

It's my birthday next week, the end of 1954 and it is time that I left home. Kitty and Charlie were younger than me when they moved out and even the twins spend more time in Nyngan than they do here now that they are working. Dad says I should be getting married and having babies but there is no likelihood of that unless Nyngan's finest bachelors are replaced with a new batch! I have been saving as much as I can of my salary from the post office. It isn't that much but enough for a train fare and four weeks rent in Sydney.

I saw a job in the Gazette for telephonists at the GPO in Sydney yesterday and I have decided that I will write an application. It will be much busier but I assume the exchange is pretty similar to the one here in Nyngan and I have been working on that for over 2 years. I'm not sure if they have party lines in the city, maybe not. I will need to write the application carefully so that I sound experienced but also eager to learn new things. I won't say anything to Mum and Dad until I have sent the application in. There is bound to be an argument if I tell them before. Last time I threatened to leave, they had the local priest come and talk with me to convince me that I should do right by my parents and stay. Granted, I was only seventeen but not so much has changed.

One good thing is that two of my friends are already in Sydney. Ivy used to work at the post office with me and she has a job at Mark Foy's in the city. It sounds very posh, she is in haberdashery and sometimes they move her to the beauty counter when it's very busy. She got the job because her uncle is a Foy, some relation of the big family I suppose. Ivy lives with Patsy who was at the bakery in Nyngan until a year ago when her whole family moved to Sydney. Patsy got a job in a teahouse in Rowe Street which I think is near the centre of the city, close to the GPO where I will be (if I get the job). The two of them live in rooms in a residential hall for young women that they say is very respectable and not too expensive. I am not exactly sure where it is but I think they can cycle to work so it must not be too far. It would be such fun being in the city, able to go to dances and cafes.

Part of me is nervous just thinking about writing the application. My legs will probably collapse under me if I actually get the job – either from excitement or terror, who knows! I don't really know the city at all. I went there once when I was visiting Kitty in the mountains. We caught the train and went shopping for the day. The best bit was having these dainty sandwiches and an ice cream spider at the cafeteria in Mark Foy's. The women were all dressed so beautifully. Kitty said they were wealthy women who lived in the suburbs and they could all afford to 'dress to the nines' because their husbands were bankers and advertising men. It was spring and I was so envious of all the pretty hats but when I saw the price tags I was astonished. It would be three months salary for me back then.

I know it will be scary and exciting at the same time but there is no alternative to leaving. If I don't escape life here I will never be the person I am supposed to be. I'll become an old spinster with shrivelled dreams and a bitter mouth.

At lunch last Sunday Dad was talking about selling the pub and moving to somewhere more fertile with plenty of rain. Other days he says he will go back to Bourke to help Ma and Pa with their business. Mum says he is always wanting to move as a way to escape. I am not sure what he needs to get away from – maybe boredom, the humdrum reality of country living and not enough money. That seems reason enough if you ask me.

I wonder how Mum escapes or maybe she thrives on routine and predictability. 'It is ordinary but safe', I can almost hear her saying. But you know, she has her own secrets. I have seen her writing poetry when she thinks no one is watching. I found a stack of them at the back of a drawer one day. Some of them were rather good, about nature and the landscape mostly. She should send them into the paper to have them published on a Saturday. She could be famous but she would hate that. She doesn't even like having her photograph taken and to be honest that is probably best because Dad doesn't like having too much competition for the limelight. That was one of the reasons Charlie left. There only room for one of them running the property.

I am going to write the application now before I lose my nerve but I need a cup of tea to settle the buzz in my head so that I can think straight.

PS. I posted the application this afternoon. Fingers and toes crossed!

So that was how Lillian had come to work at the telephone exchange. A simple letter in reply to an advertisement in the Gazette had taken her into a world that she had only read about in women's magazines. Stella wondered if it was naiveté or self-belief that had been her greatest asset in making that shift or in fact if there was any difference between the two. And yet even having made her escape as she called it, Lillian had not been able to escape the stereotype of the suburban housewife in the end. Better than being the middle aged spinster in the outback post office but Stella wondered if it had been enough.

Chapter 17

Saturday's bright sky woke Stella and she was pleased that her nagging introspection of the night before had made way for a more cheerful mood. How could it not, she thought as she sat on the balcony looking at the sunshine dimpling on harbour with a light breeze.

There were the usual chores but she wanted to spend some time booking her accommodation for her outback road trip. She had two weeks more of interviews booked and then she could take a week off. It would be mid-semester break so there would be no teaching and the weather would be cool enough to brave red dirt country.

The booking websites were not as helpful as she had hoped. It seemed that most travellers out that way were interested in powered camp sites and shearers' cabins, definitely not for her. Flipping between websites she eventually found a B&B in Gongolgon and another in Bourke township, close to the river. She figured from there she would be able to make day trips to see the landmarks that Lillian had written and talked about.

Images from other travellers on various websites convinced her that she would need to hire a four wheel drive. Her little city car would struggle on the unsealed roads, especially if there happened to be rain. Best to hire something built for those conditions and besides it would be fun to be in a large powerful vehicle on the open road for a change. Looking at the maps and distances, Stella started thinking about all the what ifs – the car got bogged, she had a flat tyre, there was a flooded causeway to cross. Some of these places were very remote and she doubted roadside assistance was going to be handy. Calming her nervous anticipation, Stella reminded herself that she did know how to change a tyre and that she would be sure her accommodation hosts knew where she was travelling and when to expect her.

There she was again, staying safe. Still outback roads probably were not the best place to change the habits of a lifetime she smiled to herself ruefully.

Time to head over to Anna's place and go to some 'open for inspections' as the real estate industry short-handedly described the set open times that properties could be viewed without an appointment. Unlike most places in the world, Sydney was greedily addicted to auctions, shunning "For Sale" as a sign of a lame property that would go cheaply. Stella blamed the convict ancestors, always ready with a hustle, taking the big gamble, convinced there was gold just around the next bend in the river.

The first apartment was the modern one that Anna liked in the brochures. The young woman presenting the apartment paid them scant attention, spending her time instead with two other couples – young, designer sneakers, handbags that had cost as much as a small car.

'Maybe she doesn't think I can afford it,' Anna was slightly offended. 'I didn't realise that you have to dress the part to be taken seriously'.

'I hate to say it but there are times these days when I think I must have become invisible. I've decided that I will use it as my superpower rather than be put off by it', Stella said.

The apartment was very smart. White and shiny, hard surfaces, enormous windows looking over the harbour, clever design features, Anna thought she could see herself in the light, clean space that it created. 'I don't want to return to the clutter of my old life. I want somewhere that says loud enough for everyone to hear, this is a new phase of life.'

The second apartment was more traditional. A beautiful old build, nice renovation, warm and welcoming. Stella thought it had more heart than the first one but Anna seemed less keen. 'There are secrets in these walls that I don't care to explore - you can almost hear the laughter and smell the family roasts. It's a happy feel but I don't want to live in someone else's past'.

'Don't you find that comforting? It makes me feel warm and welcomed, not needing to work too hard to make it mine,' Stella resisted Anna's less positive assessment. 'But you have to live here not me so let's have at look at the last place.'

Another short drive brought them to the third apartment block. Another smart young real estate agent looked them over and handed them a brochure. The building had been designed by a famous architect fifty years earlier and it was considered a landmark building in the area. The apartment was bright and spacious. It incorporated the sort of features that modern streamlined buildings avoided like entry halls and wide corridors to create an opulent generosity and grace. Stella loved it immediately. Anna was less sure but prepared to be convinced especially as she walked out onto the wide private terrace. 'This is nice. I could see myself spending a lot of time out here. It doesn't have a view like the other two but this outdoor space is fantastic. Almost like having your own backyard.'

'It will be less of an adjustment to move into somewhere like this after your current house', Stella said. 'I've been lucky with my apartment but I hear so many stories of nosey neighbours and people who complain at the slightest noise. I like that you have no one above you and no walls in common or windows that look into other people's apartments. It feels like its own space'.

'I will think about it over the weekend and maybe make an offer on the first one or this one. I know they are for auction but maybe the owners will be eager for a sure sale.' Anna said as Stella bid her good luck.

It was mid-afternoon by the time Stella was arriving at St Gertrude's to visit Pete. He wasn't in his usual spots and after a quick look around she asked the nurse if she knew where he was.

'He won't be far away,' she reassured. It is time for afternoon tea and he never misses the chance for a sweet treat. Not that you would ever know it, skinny as a bean pole'.

A few minutes later Pete came through the main doors pushing the walker that he appeared to have finally accepted as necessary. He was looking down and did not see Stella until he was well into the room. In the meantime she noticed that he did indeed look thinner and he was moving more slowly, more deliberately with a novice's concentration.

'Hi Pete, how are you', Stella greeted him. 'I've missed seeing you.'

Pete brightened as he looked up to find her face. 'Well aren't you a sight for sore eyes', he grinned. 'They told me you called in last time I was at my nephew's. That was the day I slipped on his steps and banged my knees. I've been using this trolley since'. he said, pointing to the walker.

'Let's find a seat and I will bring you some tea and cake,' Stella guided Pete to a spot in the corner, careful not to make too much fuss.

Stella was telling Pete about her research project and the women she had been talking with as he drank his tea. He seemed more inspired by the cake and possibility of a second slice than the stories she conveyed. But when she mentioned that she had spent the morning planning a road trip to Bourke, he straightened in his chair and his eyes had that alert spark that she was used to seeing. As Stella had outlined her plans, Pete nodded looking pleased.

'I can't remember if I told you before about the time I spent out west. Brewarrina, Cobar, big sheep stations then but most of them have been sold off now.'

'You mentioned it the day we went to the mountains but tell me what is it really like?' Stella asked. 'I must admit I feel out of my city depths when I think about travelling out that way alone'.

Pete thought for a moment, his gaze on the horizon now, gathering memories.

'It is beautiful in its way. Harsh, dry, land but tenaciously alive. The people are like that too. Deep wrinkles, thin lips, ruined hands, their words come slowly and their smiles even slower. But they are kinder than city folk. They know that life can be snatched away and everything you've worked a lifetime for destroyed. You take nothing for granted out there. Everything is harder, whether it's making sure you have enough water and feed for the stock or keeping the generator going. Ordinary things take longer, demand more.'

Stella had never heard Pete speak with such wistfulness. He was remembering places he loved and that, in spite of what he said, were home. Not wanting to break the spell, Stella hesitated to ask the practical questions about her trip. Instead she said, 'Tell me again about the property out near Cobar. I can't begin to imagine what it must look like'.

'That's the thing. Depending on the time of year, the time of day, the rain, it changes all the time. Impermanence in an ancient place. Some days all I could see was the orange-red soil, thin and stony under that wide sky. But after rain, the grass was the greenest you have ever seen, so tender and inviting, it clashed with the soil that had turned deep auburn. The shimmer of heat haze could be depressing day after day but when the sky was storm black with an approaching deluge, I have never felt more alive or exposed. The air becomes electric on those afternoons.'

'Jeez, listen to me, going on. Tell me exactly what you're planning.'

'Well', Stella began. 'I am still flexible but the loose plan is that I drive to Belgravia for the first night and stay with my aunt. I promised I would call in on the way. From there I will make my way to Gongolgon, maybe stay somewhere along the way it its too far for one day.'

'Gongolgon, you sure about that?' Pete looked at her like she had gone mad. 'That place really is the back of nowhere. Out on The Marra, not much to see if you ask me. Even the big sheep stations are mostly gone now. Suppose the river is pretty if you strike it at the right time. It was a dust bowl last time I was there.'

'It will probably be the same but Mum spent her early years there. The only school she ever went to was near there. I'd like to see it. From there I will go to Bourke and base myself there for a few days. I plan to go out to Enngonia and a nearby waterhole that my grandfather had the lease on. I want to visit the cemetery and the library, you know, do the family research as well. On the way home I will stop in Nyngan to see the old pub that my grandfather owned for a while.'

'You'll be fine, girl. Most of those roads are sealed so no need to stress. It's not like you'll be on a remote track somewhere. Just check with the locals if there is a lot of rain. Sometimes there will be road closures but the guys at the petrol station or where you are staying will know.' Pete was reassuring.

'I expect so', Stella passed Pete some more cake. 'Any tips for must see sights while I'm out that way?'

'Ahh well now that you ask? You have to stop at the bakery in Wellington for their old fashioned cakes. The best rock cakes and finger buns in the country. In Bourke, have a drink at the Royal Hotel and definitely eat at the Chinese place near the park. Save the best for last on the way home, stop at the RSL in Nyngan for a chicken schnitzel. I can still taste how good my last one was there.'

Stella laughed, 'Well I was thinking more about historical sites but I will need to eat too.'

Stella got up to leave. 'Take lots of photos and tell me all about it when you get back', Pete said, starting to walk slowly back to his room for an afternoon nap. It was sad to see him having more trouble getting about but he was in good spirits and his mind was as sharp as ever.

That evening she transcribed two more interviews from that week. More difficult than her first few on every level.

The first had been with Poppy, a young woman who had cancelled twice before and on the day she came was intoxicated - some sort of amphetamine was Stella's guess. So although she had told her story it could not be used as her ability to provide consent was impaired. Poppy had had a brutal home life, countless foster parents, abuse in many forms. Drugs must have seemed like a lesser evil. She said she had not eaten for a day or so and her tiny frame and matchstick legs suggested this was common. She was worried on that day about one of the staff at Mandalay 'dobbing her into social security' as she said. There appeared to be no basis for this fear, rather the current manifestation of a larger paranoia. Stella knew this story was probably true of many experiences and she wondered how she would be able to capture these cruel realities alongside those of hope.

The second woman was middle aged, maybe forty although she looked older. She said her two children had been taken from her because of her drinking. She had passed out and the oldest daughter who was ten had tried to make some dinner and managed to scald herself with boiling water. It had not been the first time there had been an accident when she was drunk. Tricia had been sober for twenty days when Stella spoke to her and she had a hearing the next day to regain custody. In the meantime the kids were with her mother-in-law. She was distraught, angry, hopeless, hopeful, repentant, defiant - all at once. So charged that she could not think straight and yet she knew she had to get it together in the next twenty four hours. Stella had the feeling she was using her as a confessional to clear her mind. Tricia didn't talk about her own past except to say she had run away from home when she was fifteen. In her view that said it all.

For both these women, there were more closed doors than choices. Stella realised she could not even imagine how life was for them. Stigma was a daily stain that coloured everything, fomenting mistrust and boring into darkness. She thought of her aunt Kitty, in love with an aboriginal man in a time when her family found it shameful, suffering from depression in a time when it was best kept secret. She had been lucky her life had not derailed like Poppy and Tricia but 'there for the grace of God', as they say.

Chapter 18

The sun was exactly at eye level as Stella wound her way through several tight bends about an hour from Eleanor's place. She was pleased she had decided to bring her own car this far and hire a four wheel drive from Dubbo but just then the extra height of a bigger vehicle would have been welcome. The morning had passed quickly as she packed a small bag and then the car with the extras that she thought she may need – water bottle, waterproof hiking boots, wide breamed straw hat, sunscreen, bug spray, first aid kit. She drove out of her garage around midday with plans to stop in the mountains for lunch so that she would reach her aunt around five o'clock.

Stella was pleased with her timing for this trip. The building repairs were due to begin that day and the guys were already assembling scaffolding as she left the apartment. At least she would miss a few days of the dust and upheaval.

As she drove she thought about the questions that Eleanor may be able to help her with but the more she mulled it over, the more she was convinced that she would not really know what she needed to know until after the trip. A case of un-known, unknowns.

In recent months, Stella had accessed death and marriage certificates for some of her mother's relatives and she could trace back to the first Australian immigrants for both her grandparents. She had a draft family tree that she would show Eleanor to see if it was the same as whatever records she had. Her detective work had revealed that Lillian's paternal great grandfather had been born in the late 1700s in Ireland and her maternal great grandfather in England some 20 years later. For reasons she had yet to fathom, tracing the female lines had proved more difficult. Perhaps the births of baby girls were less assiduously recorded by her forebears than those of their brothers. Whatever the reason, she hoped that Eleanor might know more.

It was close to six o'clock and almost dark when Stella pulled into Eleanor's driveway. She had stopped at the ubiqui-tous Thai restaurant for takeaway to save her aunt the bother of cooking. The queue and the regular dispatches of phone or-ders reassured her that she had chosen well but it also meant she was later than expected. Eleanor, however, was unwor-ried at the time as she came to the front door to welcome her. Hurrying her inside with the dual motivations of escaping the slight autumn chill and returning to the television before the ad break concluded, Eleanor told Stella to make herself at home. Stella took the not so subtle hint and planted herself on the couch to watch the quiz show throughout which Eleanor gave a running commentary that included likely answers and conspiracies about rigging the outcomes.

It was something of a relief when the show came to an end and the high pitched hyperbole of the presenter could fi-nally be muted. That crescendo of anticipation had left Stella feeling on edge and her aunt positively spry. 'Time for dinner', Eleanor said as she walked to the kitchen.

'I picked up some Thai curry on the way here. Hope that is alright', Stella said.

'That's a nice treat. I had some stew in the freezer but this will be much nicer. Is it very spicy do you think? I don't usually have spicy things close to bedtime'.

'The menu said mild, so I hope it's ok for you. I remembered that Mum was not keen on spicy food at night either. There is extra chilli in a container if we feel adventurous', Stella reassured.

'Perfect. Would you mind heating it up love. Use the saucepans down there', Eleanor said pointing to the bottom cupboards. 'I don't like using the microwave too much'.

After their meal, Eleanor offered coffee and some cake her daughter had brought over the day before. They returned to the comfortable couch and Stella was glad to rest her head on its high back and relax after a long day.

'I have done a bit of research', Stella began. 'I think I have some of the family tree and I wanted to check it with you'.

Looking at the A3 page on which Stella had drawn up what she knew of Lillian's family, Eleanor nodded as she slowly read each of the names out loud. 'Yes that looks right. There's an old bible over there on the bookcase that has some family dates in it. At the back. You can check that as well'.

The bible yielded some additional details that Stella added in black Texta like the previous entries. Determinedly permanent. When Stella looked up she found Eleanor looking at her sadly and raised her eyebrows. 'Is something wrong? You look sad. I must be bringing up memories for you?'

'No it's nothing. I am tired now that is all. Maybe we can finish this talk before you go in the morning. I need to go to bed now.'

'Of course', Stella said apologetically. 'I should not have tired you out with all these questions. Can I get you something before you go to bed?' Eleanor shook her head to say the apology was unnecessary.

Stella decided to have an early night as well. It would be sensible to be well rested before the long drive tomorrow.

It was still early when Stella walked into the kitchen next morning but Eleanor was already there with a cup of tea in front of her and the makings for toast and marmalade on the bench.

'You are up early', Stella said.

'I can't sleep-in these days. Besides, I wanted to be sure to see you this morning before you leave.'

Stella had her back to Eleanor, putting bread into the toaster when her aunt started speaking again. 'I have been putting off telling you something ever since your Mum died. I wasn't even sure I would tell you but I promised.' Stella walked slowly to the table and sat down, not sure what to expect but anticipating it was bad news from Eleanor's expression.

'When I spoke to Lillian a few months before she died she gave me a letter for you. She told me what it was about, a secret she had kept for years and didn't have the heart to tell you herself. I promised her that I would tell you what I knew but even now I can hardly believe it.' Eleanor looked into her empty teacup, seeking truth in the scattered leaves.

'Your Mum and Dad had been married about three years and they had been trying to have a baby all that time but without luck. Lillian decided she should get checked out because she had convinced herself that she might not be able to have children. She had some tests in the city at the Women's Hospital and turns out everything was fine'.

'Well of course', Stella interrupted. 'She had me'.

Eleanor nodded, 'So soon after that, Lillian came here to stay with Mum for a couple of weeks. Mum had been sick with 'flu and she wanted to help out. While she was here she met Ivan. He had a goat farm two properties further down the lane in the days before goats were trendy. Ivan was Italian, he immigrated to Australia after the war having learnt English as a prisoner of war. He liked to say he learnt English at Oxford as that was where the farm was that he worked on as a POW.

Stella nodded thinking, finally an explanation for the photo of the goat man.

'I remember Ivan from when we first came here and I always thought he was odd. I was a bit frightened of him when I was little Later I realised that his English was rudimentary when he first arrived in Australia and beside he was a loner, happier with his goats than a crowd.'

Stella sat forward in her seat, not sure where this was going.

'Lillian had started to learn to spin yarn in the mountains as a way to create amazing handmade jumpers for her and David. So when she heard that Ivan had goats she thought she could buy some of the fleece to make something for the following winter. Ivan was happy to sell her the goat hair and showed her how to clean and degrease it so as not to damage the fibre.

'Lillian took to popping in to say hello to Ivan on her daily walks along the lane. Sometimes he would be in the shed making cheese, other times she found him in the kitchen preparing pasta for lunch. All this was very exotic and Lillian loved how Italian it all seemed.

'At some stage during that visit, Lillian and Ivan became lovers', Eleanor's voice lowered as she came to the crux of her story.

'Whoa! Not really. That can't be right', Stella felt like her brain had exploded. She could not begin to imagine her mother having an affair. She and her father had been so happy together.

'Well yes, I was surprised too when your mother told me the story. Even more so when she said that they had continued to see one another every time she came to visit Mum for over two years.'

Stella's breathing was shallow and she held her face in her hands as Eleanor continued. 'Lillian also said that she was fairly sure that Ivan was your biological father. She could never be sure but she found out she was pregnant a year or so after the affair began – she had been up to see Mum a few times'.

'Did Dad know? Did this Ivan know? That I was his daughter?', Stella's voice was harsh with a rage that surprised both women.

'As far as I know, no, neither of them ever suspected that you were not David's biological daughter. Ivan died when you were a baby so if Lillian had planned to tell him there was never an opportunity.'

'But I am like Dad in so many ways. We had the same sense of humour. I love reading, just like him. I like my own personal space, quiet times, just like him. It's not possible.' Bewildered chaos gripped Stella's brain.

Thoughts crashed into each other and were lost before they were fully formed. She stuttered that it must all be a lie while

Eleanor patted her hand and let her absorb the shock. People talk about shock as a body blow, for Stella it felt more like she had been slashed in two by lightening. Stunned and burnt at the same time.

'Poor Dad. He would have been so sad if he had known Mum had been unfaithful. He idolised her,' Stella was lost, 'And you think that David could not have children, that's why Lillian was so sure I was Ivan's?'

'Yes, he was never tested but that is what Lillian believed.'

Stella walked to the sink to pour herself some water and stood holding the glass as if she had forgotten how to drink. Eleanor watched her saying nothing, remembering a saying of her grandmother, 'the air was so thick you could cut it with a knife'. Thick with anger, denial, grief.

'There is a letter for you from Lillian'.

'Why didn't she tell me herself?' Stella knew that Lillian did not lack courage. So wrong.

'I think that she had planned to but then when she became ill she could not bear the prospect that you and she would have anything between you in those last few months. She had never spoken about it to anyone until after David died. It was a deeply buried secret that she gave up reluctantly'.

Stella was adrift, too disoriented or stunned to grasp Eleanor's support. The normalcy of the dated country kitchen only intensified the feeling. Her image of her mother, her own heritage, her relationship with both her parents, all of it was a sham. Her hands were careless as they opened the large white envelope, risking ripping the single sheet of paper in Lillian's handwriting.

The words hovered, not making sense until Stella managed to slow her breathing and concentrate.

My Darling Stella

Forgive my cowardice, I should have talked to you about this a long time ago. Your Aunt Eleanor has hopefully told you some of it as she promised but you should hear from me directly too.

It's true, Ivan and I had an affair, on and off for over two years. He was so different to anyone I had ever know, so foreign. My relationship with him was nothing like my marriage to your father. More like a prolonged holiday romance, it was exciting but we both knew it was not our real life. Your Dad and I had something precious, deeper, a lifelong commitment. That was why I never dared to tell David, I feared terribly that he would leave me and that would have destroyed us both. I decided a lie of omission was the least harmful option. But I do know how wrong I was to ever have the affair, not a day went by that I did not feel ashamed and yet I could not regret it.

Looking back, I did not know Ivan very well. We had four liaisons over those years, each time no more than a few days, maybe a week. I know that he was from a small town called Moresco north of Rome. He said the family was poor after the war, work was hard to find and so he had decided to emigrate. His preference had been for Canada but Australia accepted him sooner and so he had come here. He had an uncle in Sydney who was a builder. Ivan stayed with him initially but soon opted to find somewhere out of the city where he could farm and make a life for himself.

Ivan's surname was Marinelli. I don't know anything else about his family. He was a tall thin man, wiry and brown from working in the sun. He had black curls that were always too long and slightly tangled. I have always thought that you have his hair and eyelashes. I never told him about you although I believe he heard on the grapevine that you had been born. He did not ever try to see you or contact me after we parted that last time before you were born.

The most important thing I want to say to you is that David was sincerely and entirely your father in every way that mattered. He idolised you and the two of you had a magical bond that even I would envy at times. Biology is a small part of who we are, please don't let my mistake colour how you see yourself and your father. You have every right to hate me but I am asking for your forgiveness not because I deserve but because YOU do.

All my love my beautiful girl. I pray you will find peace again after the pain that I know this news will cause you. I could not be more proud of the woman you have become. Be happy. xx

Eleanor had left the room while Stella read the letter and she returned with another cup of tea.

'Are you okay?', she asked.

Stella did not seem to hear her, 'This pilgrimage to understand Lillian's childhood now seems senseless. I did not understand her when I was with her. What do the places she grew up in matter?'

'Actually, I think it will help. Take the time to see the country. Maybe read some of Lillian's diary if you have it with you. There is nowhere like the outback. The vast emptiness can be a salve and you will have plenty of time to think on the long drive.'

Stella shook her head and walked out into the garden. How could her mother have done this to her? And that letter, so little. People say they feel gutted all the time when they have no idea of the visceral emptiness that describes, she thought, arms crossed, rubbing her upper arms.

Eleanor followed, waiting in the doorway. Her voice had a quiver, 'There was one other thing that Lillian asked me to tell you. You are one hundred percent David's daughter in everything that matters. He adored you and you shared so much in common that it was impossible to imagine that anyone else could have been a real dad to you.'

Two hours later Stella was in the car and driving west. The initial shock had dulled but she was not sure that continuing this road trip was the best idea. Still, what else was she going to do. As Eleanor said, she needed to find a way to understand the impossible and where better than in the middle of nowhere.

Chapter 19

The drive to Wellington was relatively undemanding. Not much traffic, good roads and scenery that did not draw attention to itself meant that Stella was more aware of her own thoughts than anything outside. She passed through a small town without even noticing until down the road she remember she had intended to fill up with petrol. Rashly she decided to push on to the next service centre, not really caring that she might find herself needing help if she ran out of fuel.

Her mood had shifted a dozen times. It cut her to realise she had not really known her mother as a woman. As a mother and wife her persona was uncomplicated but there had been more to Lillian. There were things that had transformed her that she had not shared with Stella and that knowledge landed as nails in the pit of her stomach. Yes, you could argue that Lillian had been protecting David and Stella from a reality that would have had bad consequences for all of them but she was also denying them a part of herself.

On automatic and yet remembering Pete's suggestion she found the bakery under the bridge as she drove into Wellington.

The next section of the drive would need her attention and so fortification with a finger bun and coffee seemed like a good idea. The finger bun had exactly the right lurid pink icing and plenty of butter, taking her back to visits to the school tuck shop. She tried to imagine the scandal if people had known about Lillian's affair, about Stella's father – the small town gossip and ostracism, David pressured by family and church to disown them, loneliness and exclusion. Her face burned as she shook her head to clear it of those images.

Whether it was the caffeine and sugar or the slap of what Lillian had spared them, her mood lifted as she wandered back to the car. Time to be back on the road for the last stretch for the day to Dubbo where she would pick up the four wheel drive.

She had avoided the temptation to make side visits to the caves, dam and zoo that beckoned from enormous billboards. Even so as she approached the outskirts of Dubbo, it was nearing five o'clock. She hoped she would be early enough to catch the rental car staff before they went home. It would be more convenient to have the vehicle ready to leave first thing in the morning. Luck was with her and a pleasant woman who could have been anywhere from thirty to fifty handed her the keys and showed her where to leave her own car. Stella was struck by how efficient and easy the whole process was compared with what she was used to in the city.

Her motel room was sparse but clean. Grey carpet, a floral quilt covering the queen bed that sagged slightly in the middle and a bathroom that could use a new layer of grout. It was fine but not conducive to occupation during waking hours - better to stretch her legs and have a look at the town.

After a short while she came to the river but turned back from the inviting riverside path as it was almost dark and the warm day was giving way to a cooler evening. After collecting a jacket from her room and asking at reception for recommendations for dinner, Stella headed out again to a local pub that the motel owner promised had 'the best steak in town'. The phrase reminded her of something her mother used to say, 'when in the country always order the steak'. She caught herself smiling at the memory and hoped it might be the beginning of reshaping her thoughts about the news from that morning.

A group that appeared to be work colleagues were deciding on what to order at a long table in the centre of the bistro area, there were two or three family groups already eating, several young men in work boots and dusty shirts were drinking at the bar and there was a competition going on around the pool table. 'Quite the hub on a Tuesday night', Stella thought, deciding to sit at the bar for a drink before dinner and to allow the activity to distract her.

The young men nodded at her and continued with their conversation which involved the merits of buying a racehorse together. Stella half listened but soon her thoughts were with her mother again. Lillian had said that civilization started somewhere east of here and yet in her diary she wrote affectionately about the landscape she had grown up in. These days nowhere was as remote as it had been then and presumably there were more job options. She was fairly sure that she had some distant relatives still living here but without names or contacts she had no plans to look them up.

As she drank her red wine, she pulled Lillian's diary from her bag and, following Eleanor's advice, to use the diary as a way to work through how she was feeling. She needed to reconnect with the mother she had known and this seemed as good a way as any although she was frustrated that the teenage Lillian was some way from becoming the woman who would have an affair. Turning to the pages after the family moved to the pub in Nyngan, Stella began to read.

23 December 1948

Tomorrow I will be 17 years old. I have been so busy since we arrived here in May that I haven't even thought of writing. I had to wipe the dust off the front cover before I started today.

I love working in the post office, sorting the mail and making sure it is packaged in bundles for Dad to take out on the run when he goes. He gets mad if I make a mistake and he has to double back or go out the Yarrandale Road a second time. He says the ruts are terrible and he had already had to replace two tyres but driving the new utility that he bought when we moved here is his new favourite pastime.

There are more people around here than there were at the lake. There's a store that keeps the basics and a school for Eleanor. The drive to Nyngan takes an hour so we go in every month to restock at the bigger stores or to go to church. The twins have started working for a cocky down the road. He has a big place and he needed more hands to help with the stock, mainly sheep but a few cows as well.

I have made some friends in Nyngan. I was nervous meeting new people because I haven't had friends my own age since I left the school when I was ten. Ivy and Patsy work in Nyngan and I see them at church and when we are shopping. Ivy works at the post office and she is learning to do the telephone exchange. Patsy is at the baker shop. Her cheeks are always rosy from the hot ovens and she has to wear her hair under a cap. She is funny and kind, always playing the clown so that everyone else feels comfortable.

Patsy has asked me to come to the New Year's Eve dance and stay overnight at her house. Mum hasn't said I can go yet but I am practically an adult so I don't see how she can say no. I have been saving up for the ticket and last week I bought some fabric to make a new dress. It's a red cotton voile and it will be perfect for a floaty party dress. I can imagine the soft swoosh as I dance around in the arms of some tall boy to Bing Crosby and The Andrews Sisters.

I am pretty sure that Mum and Dad have bought me a gramophone for my birthday tomorrow. It will be just marvellous to be able to listen to music anytime I want. I already have one record, Gene Autry singing Deep in the Heart of Texas. Kitty bought it for me when we were visiting them in Bourke three weeks ago (of course she knew what my birthday present was going to be).

Kitty and Norm aren't coming for Christmas because Kitty is pregnant and it's a long drive. I am looking forward to having a little niece or nephew. It will be fun to have a baby to spoil. Charlie isn't coming either. He is still in Queensland and Mum thinks he is going to his girlfriend's place for Christmas. Maybe he is getting serious about her. We haven't met her yet but Charlie said they would come to visit in January when he has some holidays. By then it will be over a year since we saw him and I miss him although I won't tell him that or he'll get a big head and tease me.

Summer is the best time even though its terribly hot in the middle of the day and often well into the evening.

Everyone relaxes in the shade and takes it easy over an icy drink. I lie on the day bed in the cool of the verandah and read unless I have to help Mum in the pub.

I hope there is cake for my birthday. Mum was baking today so I think she will have made me something special. I wonder if I can convince Dad to let me have a beer to celebrate. That would be a proper celebration!

5th January 1949

I was SO happy when Mum agreed to allow me to go to the New Year's Eve dance in Nyngan and it was as wonderful as I imagined. Dad drove me there on Friday morning and we went directly to Patsy house. Mum had given Dad strict instructions that he must meet Patsy's mum and check it was alright for me to stay. I packed Mum's small overnight bag for the stay, being careful that my new red dress was folded so as not to crease too much. Mum let me borrow some of her lipstick and face powder as well as the pair of shoes that she bought specially for Kitty's wedding. Lucky we are the same size.

We spent the afternoon washing our hair and getting ready. Ivy came to the house about six o'clock so that we could all walk to the dance together. I felt pretty in my new dress. It has a cinched waist which according to Mum, makes the most of my figure. I couldn't help noticing however that all the other girls were gorgeous – I felt like a small brown sparrow compared with their voluptuous figures. Still three boys asked me to dance once the music started. The church hall was beautiful, full of flowers and balloons and twinkling lights. There were sandwiches and cake for supper and orange cordial for those too young to drink beer. At midnight everyone was whooping and hollering, the boys with cars tooted their horns and then we all sang auld lang syne. I couldn't sleep for hours after we went to bed. Patsy and I top and tailed in her bed and she went off right away. I could tell from her snoring but I was wide awake, remembering every single detail of the dance.

Next morning Patsy quizzed me about the boys I danced with because she thought I might be sweet on one of them. I shook my head when she asked. They were all nice enough and one was a good dancer but all the boys from around here will work on the land or in one of the businesses in town. That's not for me. Patsy agreed, she often goes to the city with her family and she says it so much better than living here. There are dances and movies every week and everyone is more elegant and cultured.

Putting down the diary, Stella walked to the bistro counter to order steak, crossing her fingers that the chef and she shared similar ideas about what medium-rare meant. Wine or reading had left her feeling almost tranquil and she stopped noticing her heavy shoulders and stiff neck. Agitation and turmoil were not who she was.

She had never had to forgive her mother for anything and now she realized that was exactly what she needed to do. For the affair. For the secret. For cowardice. For infidelity, not only to David but to her.

The letter gave so little. Aunt Eleanor had answers to none of the questions that chased around her brain.

What might have happened if Ivan had not died when she was a baby? Would Lillian have told David about the affair? Would she have told Stella? Stella couldn't imagine growing up without David as her father. He had been so stable, so calm, always able to fix the latest drama. Never any fuss. Lillian was more prone to hyperbole and theatre. David had said he loved that about her and Stella knew that her mother had only been able to be that way because of his steadfastness. Thank goodness Ivan had not broken their marriage.

The steak arrived, perfectly cooked accompanied by a more than generous serve of fries and the obligatory lettuce leaf and slice of tomato. Definitely a meal to sustain the weary traveler. The fellows from the bar had also moved to the bistro where they were making short work of their meals and debating the likelihood of their football teams winning that weekend.

Stella by contrast chewed with slow concentration and wondered why she had so little curiosity about Ivan. Surely, she should want to know more about him. Strangely that was not the source of her most pressing questions. The enigma that Eleanor painted was enough for now. It was the secret side of Lillian that she craved more knowledge of.

The next morning, she was in her rental vehicle early, determined to make the most of the day and arrive in Brewarrina by midday. According to Google Maps it would take about four hours and her plan was to stop for lunch, visit the local library if it existed and the cemetery before driving back to her accommodation in Gongolgon.

After a couple of hours, she was approaching Nyngan and the earth had turned red and dust hung in the morning air. She would stay in Nyngan on the return journey so she kept on across the flat country. The straight line of the road with its distant mirage was mesmerizing and Stella was pleased she had decided to break up the journey. You could find yourself in a trance out here.

Brewarrina was a small place graced by the river. The man in the sandwich shop said they had had good rains at last and for once stock prices were good. The townspeople were in an optimistic stretch that no doubt would be broken by the next flood or drought. Stella ate her lunch in the shade of a eucalypt beside the river, watching a few kids splash about in the shallows and a couple of old guys fish from the bank. The noise the kids were making can't have been helpful to the fishermen but they didn't seem to mind.

After a while, Stella realized the kids were speaking a mix of English and what she guessed must be their aboriginal language. She had never heard an aboriginal language being used in this everyday way before. Sometimes at the university it would be used for welcome ceremonies but this was so much more striking, to see these young ones carelessly owning their heritage. She wished she had taken some time before she set out to learn more about the people of the area. The only tourist fact she had gleaned was that she must see the fish traps on the river which had used for centuries for fishing. Perhaps one of the fishermen could point her towards them.

Following his instructions, she went over to the cultural centre in time to join a tour. Later she mocked herself for not knowing about these amazing cultural constructions. Not for centuries, as she had been thinking, but for forty thousand years people had used this way of hunting fish. What a revelation! For the first time since she left the city, Stella found herself engrossed in the landscape. Her story was a meagre part of its history; her presence transitory; her place borrowed.

Time got away and the library was closed before she found herself outside its doors. Deciding to cut her losses, she headed back to the B&B that she had booked in Gongolgon.

She had not noticed it as she had driven through the first time but presumably it would be easy enough to find.

Presumably perhaps but not actually. Google maps and GPS were proving inadequate to the challenge of outback navigation, not something she had thought about in planning this trip. After asking at the service station and then again at a corner store, Stella found the Tarcoon Road which was lined with mulga scrub and saltbush but thankfully sealed. The low white farmhouse was ten minutes from town and she was welcomed enthusiastically by two big dogs as she drove into the front yard. It was a relief to see her host who introduced herself as Wilma not far behind. Stella wasn't convinced the sheep dogs would be terribly friendly left to their own instincts.

A quick shower to wash off the dust of the drive and Stella was happily settled in the kitchen with Wilma who was preparing dinner. Wilma told her that her husband would be home late because he had gone to Dubbo to the cattle sales. She didn't expect him for dinner so it would just them.

'How long have you lived here?' Stella asked.

'Me, about fifteen years but Jim is from here. We met when we were both studying Agriculture and eventually, he coaxed me into joining him out here. I love it now but it took a while. You can't see the beauty when you are in drought and in the first three years I wondered if anything would ever grow again. It almost destroyed me to see animals starving, their rib cages pushing through their hides, with no idea when the torture would end'.

'And eventually the rains came?'

'Yes, eventually and there have been bad droughts and occasional floods since but I am battle ready now. I've learned to see the flow of it, although even the old folks say its getting worse and that the extremes are more extreme than they used to be.'

'Because of climate change I suppose', Stella said.

'Yes, not too many climate deniers around here. What brings you here? Don't often see a woman travelling by herself unless it's for work'.

'No, not work. My mother spent her first ten years near here during the 1930s. It was the only school she ever went to and she remembered her time there fondly' Stella started to explain. 'I suppose this is a pilgrimage of sorts to better understand my history.'

'The school in Gongolon is still going strong.'

'Uh, she was at a smaller school about thirty minutes from here. It was a rail siding but as far as I can gather it's been derelict a long time. I phoned ahead for permission to access the area tomorrow. It's part of a big station now and the owners were good about letting me visit.'

'What was your mother's name? Still have relatives out this way?' Wilma asked with her back to Stella as she investigated the state of the vegetable soup on the stove.

'She was an O'Sullivan. Her father was Ted O'Sullivan and her grandfather, Charles Guthrie was a butcher in Bourke about the same time. In her diary she mentions a Mrs Evans who obviously made a big impression on her. As far as I know there aren't any relatives left around here. All of Mum's siblings drifted away, north or east.'

'It is a hard life out here and must have been doubly so then. A lot more people lived here while the rail line operated but that's long gone. Now the wealthier families have their own planes and the rest of us drive to Dubbo when we need a break.'

The evening passed pleasantly with small talk about local events and the few stories Wilma had heard from locals about what life used to be like. When Stella excused herself at nine o'clock, Jim was not yet home and Wilma was getting ready to watch a movie on TV.

Stella was tired after another day of driving and she also needed some time to herself, even after all those hours alone in the car. She could turn into a hermit out here if she wasn't careful.

Sleep took a long time to come as Stella thought back to the old house Eleanor had shown her at Christmas, her great grandparents house and the setting for Lillian's clandestine relationship. Other things came to her as well. Lillian had drunk espresso coffees after dinner when cappuccino was the normal offering and they had had real pasta with proper pesto for as long as Stella could recall. She knew this was different to other families but had put it down to Lillian's life in the city. As sleep approached an image of herself in a rough spun jumper, putting the family cat into her doll's stroller formed and she turned onto her side knowing it must have been Ivan's wool.

Chapter 20

A blue ribbon of light formed a tight angle with the bitumen which quickly gave way to a sandy track. Not hot enough yet for the sizzling shimmer to have formed and Stella felt close to her usual self for the first time since she had left Eleanor's place.

Wilma had provided rudimentary directions to the rail siding and Stella was surprised to find it easily although not much remained. There were foundations of two or three houses and a larger building that could have been the school. Lillian had described the school as opposite the siding so Stella was reasonably confident that the broken bricks suggesting a long gone long narrow building would be its foundations. The rail line was rusted and askew, well past being able to carry a freight car filled with wool.

It felt like it had been an age since anyone had been here, save the two crows that watched her carefully. A few stunted mulga bushes, bundles of spinifex, gravelly, impoverished earth, unyielding. No wonder Lillian said they had not been able to grow vegetables or raise chickens when they lived here.

Stella tried to imagine her grandmother raising her brood with a husband who was on the road more often as he was home. How had they remained cheerful, hopeful when all that Stella could see was scorched and withered?

She attached a photo to a short message to Eleanor to tell her she had found her parents old home. She knew Eleanor would be waiting to hear from her to know she was alright but phone reception had dropped out soon after she left Wilma's place so sending it would have to wait. The lack of phone coverage did play on her mind as she started towards Bourke. She had not seen any other vehicles all morning and although both Wilma and the people at her next B&B knew her itinerary things could go wrong.

It was a relief to hit the main highway again and to see more traffic. A flat topped mountain over to her left must be Mt Oxley, she remembered the tourist information she had read when preparing for the trip. Occasional citrus orchards, their dropped fruit circling the base of the trees, and irrigation channels that she supposed would be for cotton brought a diversity that lightened the landscape. After the short cross country drive, Stella was ready for a coffee.

The café was opposite one of the town's hotels, a disappointing contrast to the beautifully renovated old courthouse. Apparently, her great grandfather, Patrick O'Sullivan had owned a pub here at one time although this one was probably a later development. Lillian had not talked much about her father's parents who died when she was young. She only knew them through family stories. It was said that Patrick had run for parliament and that he had been a well off property owner until he was hit badly at the beginning of the Depression. Whatever the truth, Lillian's father was bitter that his inheritance was a pittance.

That afternoon the library provided some answers. Patrick had been an aspiring but unsuccessful politician in spite of the support of his uncle by marriage who had been in parliament in the 1890s. He had owned two hotels at different times and had a small holding out the Enngonia road. One of the pubs had burned down and the other was transferred to a new owner after only two years. He may not have been such a successful businessman after all. The maternal side seemed to be more prosperous with Charles owning a butcher shop and a small house a few streets away. He lived a less flamboyant life than Patrick if newspaper mentions were any indication. There was one short report of a court case in which he was ordered to pay additional fees to the inspector of slaughterhouses: three pence per head for sheep and pigs which according to the Local Government Act were included in the term cattle. Charles had argued that he should only have to pay fees for bovine cattle and his loss set a precedent that others would not thank him for.

Stella found the headstones of many family members including a distressing number of infants in the well maintained cemetery. Precarious times, thought Stella as she walked up and down the rows, noting down the dates, ages, maiden names, one eye on the look out for snakes. Catholic, Church of England, Presbyterian all neatly divided regardless of kinship. Eighty six seemed to be a particularly risky age with no less than six of her forebears dying at that age.

The next morning Stella headed out of town towards the lake which had been Lillian's home in her teenage years. She almost missed the sign which had fallen down and had to reverse back to the side road that took her down to the old house. A chimney, some foundations and scraps of broken china were all that remained of the years Lillian had described. There were some broken railings that may have been from the yard where Lillian used to practice her riding and a fairly intact windmill at the edge of the lake. The lake was remarkably full given the dry times and Stella wondered if Lillian and her siblings had ever swum in it. There were no mentions in the diary but it looked so inviting, cool under a hot sky. Then again, when Lillian was here there would have been mobs of sheep and cattle stirring up mud and slush, diminishing it's enticements. The only sign of life now was an old goanna lurching along the edge of the lake.

Everything thing hung in a balance dictated by heat and water. It seemed both perfectly just and terribly heartless – something Stella could believe in.

There was a sandwich for lunch and sitting under the one valiant tree near the water, she tried to imagine how growing up here had shaped her mother. It had made her determined not to stay, that was certain, and yet she wrote about it with warmth. Looking across the red, flat dirt Stella could see no boundaries, no fences, no roads. Maybe this place had more in common with a big anonymous city than Stella had every imagined – easy to lose yourself and be yourself. There was more freedom than in a small town that was for sure. Only the bull ants kept tabs on your whereabouts and the gossips were galahs and red winged parrots more intent on finding food than anything you might do.

Stella made a short detour to Enngonia before driving back towards Bourke township. Children were playing happily in the front yard of the school yard and there was a small vegetable patch on the side fence where baby lettuce and strawberries were being coaxed along. Other than a police station, hotel and small general store there was little else to see as the townspeople sensibly avoided the midday heat.

As she approached Bourke, two emus ran beside the car and Stella was both delighted and terrified. People said emus were unpredictable and these two were living up to that reputation, ready to run across her path at any minute. She was happy to see them veer away to the left and disappear into the scrub on the outskirts of town. Only as she neared her accommodation did Stella realise that she had not been dwelling on what Eleanor had told her about her mother. People are complex, even mothers and she was beginning to accept that Lillian was especially so.

Her phone beeped near town as reception was re-established, probably Eleanor thanking her for the photos she had sent this morning at breakfast when she had Wi-Fi. Time for a shower and a cold drink looking out over the river before dinner at the local Chinese restaurant as recommended by Pete.

The light had changed from the glare of the day by the time Stella walked into the bar to order her drink. There were two other women in one corner who looked like tourists. It was the three quarter cut off pants, sleeveless puffer jacket and sensible walking shoes that gave them away. Otherwise it was a male domain, locals and those passing through set apart by their choice of a table or the bar. The locals all seemed to be up one end of the bar exchanging gossip and chatting up the young backpacker who was serving drinks.

Having made herself comfortable near a window with her gin and tonic, Stella watched the depths of the river darken and a pale pink light make a path down its centre. The trees along the banks became indistinct until they were black caricatures of themselves.

Stella picked up her phone after most of the light had gone to check her messages. There was a missed call from Anna and a voice message to say that she had bought the apartment with the big terrace that Stella had liked so much. Her offer had been accepted that morning and she was phoning to say how much she was looking forward to having her own place and to thank Stella for her help.

The second missed call was from Lillian's lawyers, asking her to call back when she had a chance. That was good, probate must have finally been sorted and everything could be finalized. Maybe Anna's new place would inspire her to upgrade her own apartment with some of her inheritance. She loved the view where she was but another bedroom and larger entertaining space would mean she could have people over more regularly. She would think about it some more over the Mongolian lamb that she planned to order for dinner.

Before leaving Bourke next morning, Stella drove to the site of her great grandfather's butcher shop. It was a house now, built in the fifties she guessed and two small dogs were barking and running in the front yard. The house they had owned was also gone, the site of a school. Stella was not sure if it was the disappointment of neither building remaining or the poor sleep of the previous night that made her feel out of sorts. There had been a lot of yelling and partying long after she had gone to bed. At the restaurant, the waitress had told her it was 'pay day' and that it could be a noisy night. She had noticed people gathering in the park on her way out and thought there might be some local event. There were family groups, young people, mostly indigenous folk, sitting around eating, drinking, laughing. By 2am when she finally slept, there was a fair amount of shouting as well and she wondered for the safety in some of those families.

Stella bought petrol on her way out of town, surprised to find that she had to pay before she could pump. She supposed if someone absconded, they could go a very long way out here. She had almost forgotten to call the lawyer and decided to call from the car before getting on the road. It would only be a few kilometers before reception became unreliable.

The lawyer answered after a couple of rings, apologizing for contacting her while she was on holidays.

'That's no problem', Stella said, 'except that its impossible to predict when the phone will be in range out here. Sorry to not call you back yesterday.'

'The reason for my call was to let you know it will be a few more weeks before we can settle your mother's estate. All the bank assets have been cleared now but I tracked down that trust account number that we found in the safe deposit box. It turns out it was a different account to the one that you thought, an account that Lillian set up in 1964. It contained the proceeds from an inheritance she received from someone called Ivan Marinelli. Does that ring a bell?'

Stella did not reply immediately. 'Are you still there?', the lawyer asked.

'Yes, I'm here. Mum did know someone of that name but I had no idea she had received anything when he died.'

'The investment seems to have been pretty much un-touched since it was established. Almost like it had been forgotten.'

Not forgotten, Stella thought. Buried.

'It's for a substantial sum', the lawyer went on. 'I have to see the final figure from the bank but its in the vicinity of three million dollars.'

Stella swallowed; she had no words.

'I realise this could be a shock', the lawyer went on when she remained silent.

'There have been a lot of those', Stella whispered, not ready to engage with another revelation.

'You don't need to do anything. I just wanted to explain why the will is taking longer than expected to execute and give you a heads up on the likely size of your inheritance'. The lawyer was sounded like she wanted to get off the phone as soon as possible. Stella's reaction was not the excited one she had expected.

'Yes of course and thank you, I appreciate it', politeness kicked in but Stella was still holding the phone minutes after the lawyer had rung off. Well so much for Lillian downplaying, Ivan's importance in either of their lives. It seemed he was making a grand if late entrance and Stella had no idea how she felt about it.

The drive to Nyngan passed with disparate, agitated thoughts vying for dominance. Denial, anger, what comes next, she asked herself as she thought about how Lillian had been so important to two men. David for a lifetime and Ivan for a moment and yet she did not seem to have hurt either of them. Was that possible? Had Lillian been tempted to use the money that Ivan had left her? There had been plenty of times when things were tight when Stella was growing up. There must have been a temptation to make things easier. But she had passed it on to Stella and now she wondered if it was a windfall or a burden. It seemed ungrateful but there was something tainted in all of this. And Lillian. She was becoming more of a puzzle, one never to be solved it seemed.

As a way to distract herself, Stella thought back to those women she had interviewed at Mandalay Cottage. What would any of them have given for this sort of money? It was likely beyond their imaginings she thought. With just a little, Jenny would have been able to buy her own home, Marcia might have finally been able to access proper mental health care, Carly would have had the means to escape the bad crowd that brought her down to drugs and robbery. How could Stella not appreciate her good fortune? She decided that she would call Anna that evening. Both to congratulate her and to debrief with someone who knew her well. Someone not shy to provide advice.

Chapter 21

The pub that her grandparents had owned was close to Nyngan on the main highway. There wasn't much left, save some old stock yards and a low stone wall. Stella only stayed a while before continuing on into town to find a motel for the night.

After a walk along the main street, she found Pete's famed RSL but was disappointed to find no chicken schnitzel on the menu. Oh well, the burger would have to do. My first meal as a millionaire, thought Stella with a sardonic smile. The dining room was stark and empty when Stella arrived but the service was friendly and she tried to unwind. Keno calls over the PA and the clang of pokies jangled with her thoughts to make relaxation impossible.

She tried to imagine living in a town where this was the best option for a night out and then remembered that in Lillian's time even this would not have been here. No wonder her mother had found a way to head to the city. So cloistered, looking towards an unreachable horizon, she had finally found her own adventures in ways that Stella would never have guessed. Starkly simple lives in this interminable landscape could make a person complacent about ambiguity. So complacent that they lied to their family?

The next morning, Stella took another look around town. The post office and old telegraph exchange, the courthouse and historic railway station were much as they would have been in Lillian's day but there were few people about and a depression hung over the low buildings. Stella was glad to be heading to Dubbo to swap the rented vehicle for her own, knowing she would be at Aunt Eleanor's well before dark.

Once on the road she called Anna on her handsfree. 'Congratulations on the new apartment, you must be super excited', she said as her friend answered.

'And relieved to have a whole Saturday to myself with no "Open for Inspections" scheduled', Anna laughed. 'I was certain that they would knock back my offer so when the agent rang I was so happy'.

'Did you try for the other one you liked?'

'Not in the end because they weren't open to offers before auction and I wanted to avoid that heart stopper if at all possible. You know me, too emotional to bid myself and too much of a control freak to let someone else do it for me'.

Stella laughed trying to imagine her friend locked in a bidders war at auction. Anna had definitely chosen the right option. There was no telling how much she would have ended up paying without a cool head.

'Are you home already?' Anna asked.

'No I am halfway between Nyngan and Dubbo and finally there is more green and the trees are normal height. Somewhere near the border of the country and the outback'.

'But it has been a good trip?'

'It has been an overwhelming. The landscape, the solitude, the family history have left me wrung out. I wouldn't have missed doing it and I am desperate to return home at the same time', Stella was honest but not ready to disclose everything.

'Sounds intense. When are you back?'

'Sunday, hopefully not too late but it will depend on when I leave Aunt Eleanor's. I don't want to run away too early. She has been good to me.'

'Let's plan to catch up for dinner mid-week. I'm free most days', Anna was trying to visualise her calendar. What about we go to that new Japanese place near you? Say Wednesday after work? I can book'.

'Sounds good. You can show me photos of your apartment and tell me all the details and I will tell you about my travels', Stella wondered if the lightness she had tried for was convincing.

'Perfect. I will send you a message with the time. Drive safely, lovely'.

She rang off and because she had time, she decided she would make a detour to see the ancestral house.

The one that Eleanor had showed her at Christmas she now saw in a whole new light. The one Lillian had visited. The one where she had met Ivan. Stella walked past the house down the lane to what would have been Ivan's property. It was a hobby farm now with three alpacas and two sheep in the front yard. The house was maybe ten years old but there was an old shed behind. She wondered if that was where the goats were milked and cheeses made. The rose garden certainly must have come after the goats if what she had heard about their ravenous appetites was true.

Presumably this farm had once been Lillian's. Stella wondered when she had sold it and how she had managed it without David knowing. So many details that would remain a mystery. It was like watching one of those European movies that end suddenly with no explanations and half the plot lines unresolved. Frustratingly real.

Eleanor was already at the door when she pulled up. 'The kettles on, you must need a cup of tea after that long drive'.

'That would be perfect', Stella said, stretching her arms and back to loosen up the tight muscles. 'It's been quite a journey, the last few days, in more ways than one'.

'I can imagine. Most of my memories are from when we lived at the pub near Nyngan and then we had a couple of years in Bourke before we moved here. My clearest memories are of weather, it defined us in ways that are hard to explain. Did you like the country?'

'I wouldn't say I "liked it" exactly but it is certainly magnificent. My strongest impressions were of emptiness, remoteness but there was a lurking malevolence too. It sets your emotions on edge but you are right the one connection I did feel was to the way wind, sun and scarce water shaped life there'.

'How are you feeling about your mother now?' Eleanor asked as she place a cup in front of her.

'Better, still hurt and angry but resigned that there was a part of her that I will never fathom, never know. Sorry', Stella looked up as the thought struck her, 'I realise I have never asked you that question'. Stella frowned, brows raised in apology.

'I have had a long time and the truth is I was angry for a long time. Angry with Ellen for not telling me the truth sooner and with Kitty for abandoning me. I never knew Kitty before her mental illness but Lillian used to tell me stories of her as a carefree girl. There was envy too, of Valerie and May, just little girls at the time who had what I never could'.

'How did you move past that anger. I feel like I'm stuck with it'.

'Honestly, I'm not sure I have sometimes but I don't think about it very much these days. It doesn't define my life anymore and for the period it did I was very unhappy'.

'My relationship with Mum and Dad has been a big part of who I am, maybe because I haven't married. Mum was an important influence and now she is gone and it's as if she never was. Well never quite as I thought anyway'.

'All of us have a little that we don't reveal. She was not so different in that. She always lived larger than where she was and her secrets, too, were more rattling than most. Lillian was the strongest woman I knew but she wasn't perfect'.

Stella nodded, 'I think that is the thing I am having most trouble dealing with. She was strong and yet she took the easy way out by keeping all this secret. The rationale about not hurting anyone is all very well but she was cowardly too and that is something I never expected from her.'

'Me either but as they say, put yourself in her shoes. You might do the same thing.'

It was impossible to know.

'Anyway, there's more'. She didn't meet her aunt's eyes. 'Yesterday the lawyer called to tell me that Lillian's estate is much more valuable than we knew. Apparently, Ivan left her a substantial sum and it had been invested, untouched all these years'.

'Truly! I had no idea', Eleanor said digesting the news. 'Oh dear, she really must have wanted to scrub out any mention of Ivan. Deny he ever existed. How do you feel?

'Uncomfortable is one word for it. Not quite ill gotten gains but ....', Stella's voice trailed off.

'Understandable but don't be too hasty. The thing that plays on my mind most as I get older is that Ellen and Kitty's secrets meant I never knew my father or his family. I'm part indigenous but I have no connection to my grandmother's family – that's unfair'.

'I hadn't thought of that when you told me your story. Did you ever try to look them up? You said she was from Enngonia?'

'Yes Enngonia. Actually it was Tracy, my eldest grand daughter who found the family, not long before she moved to New York. Most of them live in Dubbo now and all the cousins of my generation have passed on'.

'Sad you didn't meet them. I can't say I feel very curious about Ivan's family yet'.

'Such a lot to take in, it may come, it took me a long time. Have a shower and relax while I heat up the casserole that Liz dropped over this afternoon'.

Stella stood under the shower and let everything she had heard and seen over the past week wash over her. Her past, her story were changed but she was the same person. Her mother was the same person, her father was still David. Ivan was a dim shadow. He and Lillian started this story but it was her choices that would determine how it ended.

By mid-afternoon the next day Stella was home in her apartment, unpacked, washing machine on. She was pleased she had had the forethought to take Monday off work as she felt she needed to pull herself back from the brooding thoughts of the past week. She was weary too, from the driving, the thinking, the shifts in her sense of self. Maybe she should have gone to Fiji instead and come back tanned and terrific!

One thing that she had not expected on her return was the daily reminder of the outback. The repair work on her apartment block was creating clouds of fine red dust that had settled on every surface. She had wiped everything down two and three times and still her dusting cloth collected pink silt. Lillian seemed determined to stay front of mind.

Chapter 22

Stella drove directly to Mandalay Cottage. She had spent the day before sorting out a few urgent matters at Uni and was pleased to be back helping out with volunteering and talking with the women. The rain had started before first light, heavy and consistent enough to mean the same few spots were flooded. Why doesn't the council sort that out, Stella wondered for the hundredth time as she saw a woman walking her dog drenched in the wake of a thoughtless driver.

Later in the week she would need to take stock of her research so far and collate the stories into a manageable order but today she just wanted to talk and listen. No agenda, a re-acquaintance with a difficult world.

The boss, Rosemary Benton was talking to a client near the entrance when Stella arrived. As she got closer, Stella recognised Jenny who had volunteered for the first interview. She was about to call hello when she realised that she was crying and there was blood on her face and clothes. Worried, Stella hung back, not wanting to intrude but anxious to help if she could. She had been so please to have her own home when they last talked. Stella hoped that nothing too terrible had happened, imagining that the Ex- may have reappeared.

Rosemary was walking Jenny over to a chair when she saw Stella. 'Jenny has been in an accident Stella, do you think you could sit with her for a minute? I need to find our first aid person and we might need to take her to the GP clinic'.

'What happened?' Stella asked looking at Jenny's nose which was bloody and at an angle.

'I was walking around the corner on my way here. It was supposed to be my first shift as a volunteer and instead I seem to be a client again'.

'Were you mugged or something?'

'No, I had my umbrella low over my head to stop it turning inside out and I didn't see the food delivery guy coming towards me on his bike. He was really moving, trying to avoid the rain as well but on the footpath as they all seem to be these days. He swerved at the last minute but crashed into my left shoulder. It felt like a thunderbolt and I hit my nose on the back of his bike as I fell. Do you think it's broken?'

'Looks like it? And your lip has a decent size cut as well. I can take you down to the doctor after they have cleaned you up a bit. You should have some water', Stella said digging a water bottle out of her tote bag.

'Thanks. I do feel a bit dizzy and my heart is racing. The adrenaline I suppose'.

'Take it easy', Stella said as Rosemary returned.

'Our senior first aid person is actually with another client. They are waiting for an ambulance and she will be tied up for a while'.

'Do you think you can walk to my car?' Stella asked Jenny.

'Yes, so long as I take it slow'.

'Let's take you down to the GP clinic then and see is someone there can fix you up'.

'Thanks Stella. I can call ahead to let them know you are on the way. Call me if you need anything', Rosemary said.

The doctor's surgery was quiet and Jenny was seen almost immediately. By the time she left, she had a piece of tape over her nose and a stitch above her lip as well as two rapidly blackening eyes. A couple of people turned to look presumably noticing the blood on Jenny's clothes but most did not even glance at them as they made their way back to Stella's car.

'Do you need anything from the Pharmacy before I drop you home?' Stella asked.

'Is that alright? I don't want to be a nuisance but I am not sure that I'm up to the bus.'

'Don't be silly. You are definitely not getting the bus. I thought you might need some painkillers or something as well'.

'The doctor offered me a script for oxy but I told him I have some paracetamol at home, that will be fine. I can't remember if I told you that I had a problem with painkillers, started taking them after a couple of beatings from Jim and it got out of hand. I don't want to go back there'.

'No I don't think you talked about it but agree better avoided. What about a cold pack?'

'Never found better than frozen peas. No, I'm all good we can go straight home'.

As they drove Jenny was staring out the passenger window and Stella assumed her face was hurting now that the adrenalin rush had passed. However as she turned Stella could see that she had been crying.

'Sorry, I didn't mean to cry. Feeling sorry for myself.'

'I'm sure its really painful', Stella began but Jenny interrupted her.

'No it's not the pain. I've had worse. It's the looks. You know there are two types of men in this world. The ones who look away embarrassed when they see a bashed woman and the others who smirk in that knowing way like they get off on it'.

'Really, you mean that some men find it exciting?'

'Who knows but I feel like they're leering. I had forgotten how demeaning it is. Makes me want to throw up.'

'You mean just now, those people who passed us? Shit I had no idea'.

Jenny nodded. After a minute she said, 'Remember when you were first preparing for your research and you wrote up some questions? You wanted to ask what one thing would have made a difference. For me, the one thing would have been to have more people really see me. To look at me as an equal human being. You have no idea how rare that is'.

There was nothing you can say to that, Stella thought, letting the silence and a squeeze of Jenny's hand make do.

Stella left her phone number but Jenny insisted she would be fine. She would take it easy for a day or two until the swelling and bruising eased. Hopefully she would be in better shape by next Wednesday so that she really could start that first shift as a volunteer at Mandalay.

As she drove to her office for afternoon meetings with her post-grad students, Stella was thinking about how much Jenny had experienced. And people talk about resilience, she thought. They had no idea.

That evening she changed quickly and made her way to the Japanese restaurant to meet Anna. A quick text to Jenny reassured her that she was okay and she was looking forward to catching up with her friend. Even so, she could not shake the feeling that her life was insubstantial, that she was an imposter.

Anna was uncharacteristically early, already seated and reading the menu when Stella arrived a few minutes before their reservation.

'The pilgrim returneth', she laughed standing up to hug Stella.

'It was a long trip but worth it. Good to see where Mum grew up. I can't truly imagine what it was like for her and my grandmother but it definitely must have been tough. That country is not forgiving. Everything is laid bare out there.'

'It doesn't sound like a place I need to visit anytime soon.'

'No, it's beautiful, extraordinary. You see nature in a way that isn't possible in the city. Definitely a good place to visit', Stella had given a more negative impression than she intended.

'If you say so. For now I have enough on my hands getting ready to move into the new place. The settlement is a short one which suits me but also adds to the pressure to tie up all the loose ends I've been procrastinating about'.

'Such as?'

'Oh, you know, throwing out things I haven't used or worn for years. I have more kitchen gadgets than anyone needs. There is linen that the girls might want but otherwise I will donate to charity. I must have ten tablecloths for the old dining table but as I'll have something smaller in the apartment I don't need them. It's endless'.

'Careful you are starting to sound like a minimalist!' Stella teased.

'Hardly, there will still be more stuff than can possibly fit in the new place. I need your incisive eye to come and help me decide what else needs to go'.

'Of course, just let me know when. I know someone who has just moved into new housing after being homeless for a bit, she might be able to use some smaller pieces of furniture. I can ask.'

'That would be good. I could try and sell some of it but it's not worth much and I would rather give things to people who can use them. It seems to shame for stuff to end up in landfill.'

The waiter came to take their order and to bring the wine that Anna must already have ordered.

'Before I went away you were about to go out with Steve, weren't you? How was it?', Stella asked.

'You were right. Definitely a player but we had a nice night and it was good for me to go out. I am thinking of it as a practice run'.

'He will be disappointed', Stella said. 'Or at least he ought to be.'

'I don't think so. He was probably as relieved as I was when it was time to go home. I hope we stay friends. He's a nice enough guy, just not my type. What about you did you find yourself a burly pastoralist on your trip'.

Stella laughed, 'Heavens no, that was the last thing on my mind'.

'You sounded like there had been plenty to absorb on the phone the other day', Anna waited a cocked her right brow inviting Stella to continue.

'That's one way of putting it. The whole thing was surreal'.

'So yes, the country and the family history were all absorbing but that's not what left me reeling. I stayed the first night with my aunt and she gave me a letter from Mum after telling me what she knew about an affair my mother had'.

'Your Mum, really. Did you have any idea?'

'None and apparently no one had known, not even Dad. It went on for several years, whenever my Mum visited her parents. This guy, Ivan, had a farm near them'. Stella took a deep breath. 'Mum thought that I was Ivan's child. She was fairly sure that my Dad was infertile but it was never proven'.

'Shit. And you had no idea? She never told you?

Stella continued on after the food arrived and they had started eating, 'She said in the letter that she didn't have the courage. I don't know. I suppose she did not want to ruin her marriage, she loved Dad and would not have wanted to lose him. It seems she wanted both, the certainty that Dad provided and the exotic alternative of Ivan'.

'What a way to start your trip! It must have been lonely, processing all of that and driving endless kilometres '.

'It was but it also gave me time to think and even to start to forgive. I'm a fair way off understanding yet but this is part of who Mum was. As much a part as any other. I have to respect that I suppose'.

'Hmm but you don't have to like it', Anna said.

'So that was the first twist. The second one came when Mum's solicitor called me about the will. I thought she must want me to sign some things but turns out she had found another trust account. Ivan had left her his estate when he died. My aunt said he died soon after I was born, so early 60s. The money sat untouched all that time, earning interest and accumulating. It seems I will inherit something over three million dollars from my mother.'

'Fuck. Really? That's amazing'.

'I know but I don't feel good about it. I know that is not rational but it feels wrong. Like I don't deserve it or maybe that if I take it then I am legitimizing that relationship that I didn't even know about'.

'Or maybe you are over thinking this. Your mother wanted you to have that inheritance. Use it well. Do her justice. Don't make any rash decisions'

'I don't know. It's a few more weeks before everything is finalized and as you say I don't have to do anything in a hurry. Lillian certainly didn't feel any need to'.

'It's like your Mum is having one final hand in your life from the grave'.

'Exactly and I am not sure I like it'.

'If she had told you all this when she was still alive, do you think you could have fallen out? That would have been terrible', Anna said.

'We would definitely have argued and yes I might have been angry enough to cut her off. What I am finding hardest to forgive now is that she didn't give me a chance to really know her. To see her as she really was, a woman of many facets', Stella said thinking back to Jenny's words earlier that day.

'None of us know our mothers like that. My girls certainly know me well but there are hidden corners and nooks that I don't choose to share with them That's normal'.

'I suppose so but the nooks that Lillian hid were bigger than most. Anyway, this is all still too raw for me to be reasonable. I'll get there. You know me, always better at reframing than confronting negativity', Stella laughed at herself.

'We all cope in our own way. If it were me and my girls all that I would ask is for them to judge me kindly and remember that I love them above everything else'.

'Thanks Anna. Wise words as always. Let's look at the dessert menu and talk about something else. What do the girls think of your new apartment? Have they seen it?'

'Only the pictures. The tenant has until next week to move out. Hopefully then the agent will be able to take me back for a visit to measure up some spaces. I will take the girls then if they are free. I have decided I want a new sofa and bed as well as a dining table that's the right size. I'll keep some of the pieces from the old house but I want this to be my place not a random selection of what Rex and I bought together'.

The women continued to discuss the decorating decisions that Anna had been mulling over. Paint and floorboards were altogether safer topics of conversations than the nervousness both felt as they faced new phases in their lives, not of their own making.

Chapter 23

Over the following couple of weeks she settled back to her usual routine, university at the beginning of the week and Mandalay for interviews from Wednesday on. She had almost enough material to start reviewing and analysing but she wasn't in any hurry to finish up talking with the women. These later interviews were more challenging and some of the women were at a high risk of harm. It was frustrating not to be able to do more, a sentiment with which Mandalay staff were all too familiar and one that she was coming terms with.

She had been particularly distressed by her encounter with Carly one Friday morning. She was giggly, talking too fast and too loudly. Her hair was a tangled knot and the t-shirt and jeans she wore were both inadequate for the cold, wet day and streaked with mud. One the staff made a comment about the strength of whatever had been on the street last night. It appeared she was using again, if she had ever stopped, and presumably sleeping rough. Naively, Stella had hoped she would have returned to her mother's place, but not this time. She had teamed up with a young guy that Stella had not seen there before – droopy eyes, sores on his face and arms, skin and bone. It did not look like a good pairing, she thought.

She had an interview organized that day with another woman. Mary was young, sixteen or seventeen and she had bounced around foster homes for the past two years. She implied neglect or abuse but was loath to talk in detail. She had dropped out of school a few months before and was staying at a refuge down the road from Mandalay. While she talked, she looked around constantly, checking for eavesdroppers. Her mother was in gaol and her father had left them years before. There had been a plan for her to stay with her grandmother but she had got sick with cancer and so it had been foster care. She had no friends at school, her teachers had few expectations of her, belief and trust seem to have long deserted her.

She had been trying to get enough money by begging in the city mall. 'People look straight through you. Sometimes they throw a few coins at me. I'm lucky to make twenty bucks a day', she told Stella.

'Does the refuge provide food?', Stella asked, realizing it was probably as stupid question.

'There is a kitchen but I don't cook, usually just buy a hamburger or a pizza if I have money. Otherwise dinner is a can of coke. Some nights there is a van with free food near here, usually soup or stew and that's pretty good.'

'What will you do when you leave the refuge?' Stella wondered.

'I have been to Centrelink but going for job interviews is impossible. Besides, who is going to employ me, looking like this', she said looking down at her soiled top and short denim skirt. 'One of the other girls at the refuge is going to introduce me to her cousin. She runs a place up the street'.

'You mean like an escort place?' Stella said looking for a word other than brothel.

'Yeah, I guess so.'

'When does you Mum get out of prison?'

'Later this year but I don't want to see her for a while. She's bad news, too much booze, always bringing home creeps who want more than just my Mum. I might as well get paid for it'.

The conversation was circular – much like Mary's life, Stella reflected later. It was a relief later that afternoon when Stella saw she had an email from her colleague Kirsten asking if she had time for a drink after work. No such escape for Mary, no exit from her hell any time soon.

As it happened, Kirsten had invited Stella to the pub to ask her advice about a promotion interview she had the following week. They talked about her research output and publications. She had written a new course for third year students and had good feedback. Stella told her that her chances were strong. They talked about who would be on the panel, their particular interests, tricky questions. Stella had answers and questions that were meaningful. She knew how to mentor, how to support someone like Kirsten, someone not so different to herself. If only it was so easy for the clients at Mandalay.

It was three weeks since Stella returned from her holiday and she was feeling guilty that she had not been to see Pete, to show him the photos as promised. Saturday was booked out with a dentist appointment and chores so it would have to be Sunday. She decided to call ahead and invite him out for Sunday lunch. Somewhere with a nice roast.

Pete was ready as usual when she arrived close to midday. Stella wondered if he had always been so punctual or if he was more eager these days for any variation in his routine. Given his laconic manner she suspected the latter.

'I booked a table for us at a pub about five minutes from here. They have a Sunday roast special Is that OK?', she asked.

'Pub sounds good, roast sounds even better', Pete looked pleased. He had replaced the walker he used on her last visit with a stick which he wave about as a punctuation device more than he relied on it for balance. It was good to see the improvement.

Their table was by the window and the low winter sun was in Stella's eyes as she sat down. 'Here come around onto this side, I won't bite', Pete said.

'Thanks, yes it's that or sunglasses', Stella laughed using her hand as a visor and moving to sit beside Pete.

'Besides, its noisy in here. We can hear each other better this way.'

Stella pulled her phone from her bag and opened the folder with her holiday photos for Pete to see while she went to the bar to order the food and drinks. Pete wanted the roast beef and Stella the pork, both plates arrived heaped with vegetables, Yorkshire pudding and gravy.

'These pictures of Brewarrina, they're real good', Pete complimented her. 'Takes me back to when I was working around there, shearing. There's a big station that used to hire a lot of hands, looked after us, good quarters, good grub.'

'You really love it out there, don't you?', Stella said.

'Best country. You can't tame it. The cotton guys have tried and all they do is ruin it for everyone. Take too much water'.

'People told me that the rivers are struggling. There had been good rain before I went so they were looking better but even so there were stories of salination and fish dying in the local papers. That pretty purple weed in the river is a pest that's causing damage too'.

'Water hyacinth', Pete nodded. 'It clogs everything, sucks out the oxygen. Where's this he asked holding up a photo of the lake'.

'My grandfather had the concession on that water hole in the early forties. Mum said that there was always water then but according to the records in Bourke library it's an ephemeral lake. And this one is the remains of the pub they owned. Only foundations left but it was a low wooden building - public bar, five bedrooms, an office that doubled as the post office and a big kitchen that was semi-attached. There was a photo of the original in the library, stupidly I didn't think to take a copy'.

'Your grandfather must have been an interesting fellow. Those depression years brought out the best and worst in people by all accounts'.

'From what Mum has told me, he wasn't an easy man. Always looking for the next thing. Up-rooting the family when a new chance was in the offing. Never quite succeeding but not exactly failing either. I never had the impression that Mum was close to him but she must have been'.

'It was different then. Fathers weren't expected to raise kids, that was the mother's job. Men worked, brought home enough money to feed the family and maybe went to the pub or the races on Saturdays. If they were god fearing they might go to church on Sunday with the family'.

'I remember when you told me about your time in Cobar you said it was a special place. You obviously felt close to it. I thought I might feel the same, visiting the places my family had come from'.

'Best years of my life were out west. That red dirt gets under your skin in more ways than one. What I really liked was that I felt I belonged there. Not sure why, I wasn't from there but it felt like home. But you know the locals only ever saw me as a blow in even after years of living there. And in the end, turns out they were right', Pete said.

'To be honest, there was no connection, only curiosity, a sort of intellectual interest. My grand parents endured that country, my mother left it for another small town and I am so far from it in the city that I see it but don't feel it. Seems a shame but perhaps our family have been on a journey ever since Martin O'Sullivan arrived from Dublin two hundred years ago'.

'Your lot doesn't set down roots by the sounds of it. You're like the scion on one of those grafted plants – good fruit and flowers but terrible roots. Me, I'm the opposite. The country is in me. ', Pete was uncharacteristically philosophical.

Stella frowned, wondering what on earth a scion was. She supposed it was the top bit of the grafted plant. 'Let's order some dessert', she said seeing him eye the Bomb Alaska arriving at the neighbouring table…

'Now you're talkin. What do you think that one is?' Pete asked with a nod.

'Pretty sure it's the Bomb Alaska. It's that or the cheesecake. Shall we take one of each?'

Dessert in hand, Stella returned to find Pete looking out the window. 'Tony, my nephew called me yesterday. Bindi is getting bad, can't walk much anymore. The vet said we should put him down. I know it is best but feels like a betrayal after all these years'.

'Oh Pete, I'm so sorry to hear that. What's wrong with him?'

'He's old, waterworks don't work anymore, has trouble walking. Sounds like me', Pete said.

'Maybe you can have one last day with him. Lots of cuddles and treats to say goodbye'.

'Yeah, that's a good idea. I'll talk to Tony'.

Hardly an uplifting lunch Stella thought as she arrived home mid-afternoon. Surprisingly, Pete had seemed chirpy as he left her to go and find his usual spot in the garden and afternoon tea. How that man was so skinny was a mystery.

Stella planned a quiet night in as usual for Sunday. Time to ready herself for the week ahead, maybe a long bath, a book and a glass of wine. Nothing too fancy.

She certainly was not expecting the call from Rosemary Benton from Mandalay suggesting an impromptu dinner. They agreed to meet at a local Italian place at 7:00pm and Stella felt a tightness in her stomach as she wondered what it could be about.

Rosemary was wearing her usual business attire, neat skirt and blouse when she arrived. 'I had a Board meeting this afternoon and then a meeting with a potential donor she offered gesturing by way of explanation. No time to change, sorry'.

Stella smiled and nodded, 'You really do work seven days a week'.

'Not usually but I go on leave on Wednesday and there were some loose ends to tie off. The Board are all pro bono so Sundays suit them. Its only a few times a year.'

Stella nodded again and shifted in her seat before sipping on the water in front of her. This definitely wasn't a social catch up.

'You must be wondering why I asked to meet', Rosemary began and without waiting for Stella to respond she went on. 'You seem to be doing well with your project. I have seen you interviewing several women over the last few weeks'.

'Yes, I have twenty interviews that I can use. I was planning to take a break to analyse the data to see if there are gaps I need to fill'.

'Ah, that might be a good idea'. Rosemary seemed set for one of her trademark silences when she continued, 'You see we have had a complaint or at least one of the Directors was approached by someone who was unhappy about the work. He only told me this afternoon and I wanted to speak to you straight away particularly as I'll be out of town for a couple of weeks.'

'Oh no, I'm so sorry. I had no idea - I haven't had anyone complain directly'. Stella grasped her left hand firmly with the right to stop the tremble she could see from the corner of her eye. 'A few women have chosen not to go through with the interview but that is not unusual. No one has asked me to stop or anything like that', Stella was thinking back over the people she had spoken with.

'It was a young woman you spoke with last week, well educated, good family but has had some issues with mental health and substance abuse. She told the director that she was unhappy about the interview because it was all one way. She was giving, giving and as usual the other person was taking.'

Stella sat back in her seat and exhaled, biting her lip in thought. 'Well she is right, of course. These women have been giving me their stories and I have given nothing in return except to remind them about Mandalay services that could help. All I am offering is to portray their stories faithfully and make use of the data. I can understand why that may not be enough.'

'Do you remember the interview?' Rosemary probed.

'I am assuming it was with the girl who called herself Natalie for the research. She is the grand daughter of people who arrived from Vietnam by boat in the 1970s. Her father was a small child at the time when his entire family immigrated and her mother was born in Australia to a young couple who had married immediately before sailing. Her grandparents made a living sewing and cleaning houses but both her parents went to university. Her Dad was an IT expert and her Mum is a pharmacist. They married young and Natalie is their only child – bright, she won a scholarship to a selective high school.

'She said that that was when things had become difficult. Suddenly, she was near the bottom of the class. An April baby she was younger than most of the others and found it hard to make friends. Her father died suddenly when she was fifteen and from then on it was just her and her Mum. She talked about how she used to feel anxious, unable to sleep when she had an exam or an assignment due. Her mother worried she wasn't studying hard enough and organized coaching.

'Then Natalie discovered that if she had a few mouthfuls of vodka from the drinks cupboard that the nerves went away. Later she found prescription pain killers. People would return unused medicines to the pharmacy when someone in the family died and there was often strong painkillers in the brown paper bags that sat waiting for her Mum to check and dispose of appropriately. Natalie became good at being in the right place at the right time.

'Natalie's Mum found out and sent her to rehab but she checked herself out after a couple of days. She has only been living in a refuge for a short time but she seems at a loss about what she will do now. She has had a very protected life and it must be terrifying besides she needs treatment for her anxiety and substance misuse'.

Rosemary nodded and waited for Stella to go on. 'I suppose I knew she was looking to me for answers and I did not even acknowledge that. As you know, I can't provide advice but I should have said that I understood she was looking for solutions but that I wasn't the right person to give them'.

'Yes, it's possible that in spite of all your careful listening she felt unheard. She was asking for help and you had nothing for her'.

Rosemary continued after another pause, 'From what you say and also from what the staff have told me about your volunteering I don't think there is a fundamental problem with the research and how you are handling things. I will contact the director and explain and I will also be in touch with the young woman to see how we might help her.'

'Would you like me to speak to her as well?' Stella was keen to clear the air with Natalie.

'Leave it for now. It's for "Natalie" to decide if she wants to talk to you again. I will offer it to her as an option. Assuming there is no more to the complaint when I speak to her directly you can go on with your work.'

'That awful expression, "paying it forward", doesn't have much meaning when you are vulnerable and need help, does it?' Stella said, not tasting the pasta that she had ordered absently.

'We are always asking those with least to give most, it's the way of the world, much as I hate to say it. We try to balance that but we are woefully inadequate to the task most of the time'.

Rosemary and Stella parted not long after, both needing to think about what they had heard and prepare for a busy week. Stella was restless when she arrived home, walking and up and down thinking about how she had mishandled the interview so badly. But it was the sense that she was using these women that was causing her most distress. She would benefit professionally, Mandalay would receive the research fee that was negotiated at the beginning of the project, other academics and policy people would use the results to further their own work, the women themselves would get nothing of substance. It did not seem right.

Chapter 24

Having decided to only do two volunteer shifts for a week or two, handing out clean clothes and blankets now that it was colder, Stella spent more time in her office at the university. It was weeks since she had been around on a Friday, when most of the social activities seem to happen and she realized how much she had missed the company of her colleagues. The professor who had been her doctoral supervisor invited her for lunch and Steve and Kirsten as usual were organizing drinks in their office for late afternoon.

Over lunch Stella told her old friend about the complaint at Mandalay and the more vexing question of how to avoid exploiting her research subjects.

'That's why your research went through an Ethics Committee. You have to trust the process to a point. The most important thing is that you are totally honest with the women about what is in it for them and everyone else. Informed consent has been well honed in the medical field because the adverse events can be spectacularly catastrophic but as you know not all catastrophes are obvious to outsiders'.

'I suppose so and it's not like I have never thought about this. More a case of this being about a person I spoke with and thought I understood and yet I got it so wrong'.

'None of us is perfect. Give yourself some slack and just make sure you learn from it. That's the best you can do this time.'

'Thanks Prof. It's been a hard week. Must have been showing more than I thought.'

'Not really, I hadn't seen you around for a bit and I miss our talks. I always learn something from you too you know. Take care. I have a student coming to see me in ten minutes. I think he is going to discontinue and I'm hoping to change his mind.'

'Good luck and thanks again'.

Stella returned to her desk feeling better than she had all week. There was nothing in their conversation that she had not told herself a dozen times but saying and hearing it aloud made it more convincing. She had a few clear hours to look through the transcripts she had collected so far and get on with analysing them.

The knock at her door was soft enough but so deep was she in her work that she startled with a small gasp, holding her hand to her mouth. 'Come in', she called expecting it was the student she had been talking with earlier in the day who was having trouble with a new concept.

Natalie hesitated after opening the door, 'Is it okay for me to come in?'

'Of course', Stella said apologizing for not opening the door, half explaining about the student she was expecting. Natalie came in slowly, looking uncomfortable, frowning as the words tumbled from Stella.

'This is my mother, Agnes', she said turning to draw in the older woman who had stayed in the corridor. Her quiet demeanour gave Stella pause, defusing the tension that she had felt building.

'Welcome to you both', Stella began again. 'I have been thinking a lot about you this week and I am so pleased to be able to see you. Thank you for finding me'.

'That part was easy, you are listed on the Uni's website. I wanted to come to apologise for making a complaint about you. Mum said it might have been bad for your research'.

Stella made to interrupt but Natalie raised her voice to ensure she would be able to finish her piece. 'I know you told me all about the research at the beginning and I agreed to tell my story. Actually I really liked the way you just listened and let me tell it my way but I was feeling so scared that day. The refuge had told me I would have to move on and I had already tried two other places that were full. I was afraid I would have nowhere to sleep that night. I was angry with you for not fixing that for me'.

'And I knew you were looking for more from me and I didn't go there on purpose. I should at least have let you tell me the problem so that I could suggest who could have helped. I was in a hurry to get away and I broke our conversation before you were ready. That wasn't fair and I'm sorry'.

Agnes was watching her daughter carefully and raised her eyebrows with the tiniest tilt of her head to urge her on. 'Dr Benton came to see me on Monday at the new hostel that I found. She was really kind but she was also pretty tough laying out my options. It was like she gave me a good shake without even touching me. I decided after talking to her to call Mum'.

Stella looked at Agnes who had a faint smile now. 'I was so relieved to hear from her. I wanted to hug her and smack her at the same time. We have a lot to work through, including reporting the theft of patient's unused medicines from the pharmacy. I should have had a better process in place to make that impossible and there may be consequences for me as well. We'll do this together'.

Stella finally said goodbye to the two, filled with admiration at their courage and gratitude for their generosity. They were obviously close and hopefully that would sustain them.

Feeling lighter than she had all week, Stella did a final check of her emails before she collected her things and walked over to Steve and Kirsten's office. There was an email from someone called Lena at a University of Hamburg email address. Laura! She was doing well with her new supervisors, had settled into life in Germany and so far had heard nothing from her Ex. Stella clapped her hands unselfconsciously, with a mixture of happiness and deep relief for Laura. Sometimes good people did win.

She could hear laughter and chat from the corridor, as she approached Steve and Kirsten's office - it seemed today they had attracted a bumper crowd. It soon became clear that the surprise announcement that their head of school was going to a job in the UK had spurred many into gossip mode. Not inclined to get involved in office politics tonight, Stella had a quick drink, said hello to some people she had not seen for a while, promised to have lunch with Steve soon and was about to leave when someone called her name.

There was a man asking for her at the front admin desk. Curious, at this time on a Friday, Stella thoughts as she walked quickly down the long corridor juggling bags and books.

Chapter 25

A heavy set man with dark hair was sitting on the bench as she approached, not anyone she recognized. 'Hello', her voice was hesitant as she introduced herself. 'I believe you asked to see me'.

'Yes, thanks for coming so quickly', he smiled warmly, oozing confidence and charm. 'I'm looking for an old friend who I think might have worked with you. Her name is Laura Nowak.'

Alarm bells. Stella hoped she wasn't blushing as she shook her head. 'No, I'm sorry I don't know anyone by that name'.

'She could have been a student. Someone in Melbourne thought she had moved to your department'.

'Sorry but I really don't know the name. The university has records of student, you could check with them', crossing her fingers that the records had been amended as the university promised.

'I tried that already but they were no help'. The charm was evaporating as his frustration grew.

'Well I'll ask around and if anyone knows her, I can send you a message.'

'Sure', he handed her a card, turning quickly to leave. Andre Nowak.

Stella sat on the bench until her breathing slowed. How weird that he come today when she had just heard from Laura. Was it simple a coincidence? She had never really believed her own safety could be at risk.

Later, having reassured herself that Laura's husband was no threat, Stella reread the letter from her mother about Ivan. She still felt disconnected with the woman in that letter although no longer angry with her. Perhaps Anna was right, understanding her mother in that way was not ever realistic.

Picking up Lillian's diary after what felt like forever, Stella turned slowly to some entries that she had not read yet. She didn't have a reason for not starting out at the beginning and reading through in a logical manner. Maybe the extended periods of silence between some entries had put her off or maybe it had more to do with her habit of starting at the end. All about the destination, not the journey as far as Stella was concerned. Either way, it was coming up a year since her mother's death, she really needed to finish the last couple.

10th March 1949

Ever since New Year's Eve I have been thinking that I should try to get a job in Nyngan. Dad is starting to talk about moving again and as usual Mum is trying to talk him out of it. They don't really have the money at the moment and Eleanor is still little so I think it won't happen soon.

Ivy's family is moving to the city next month because her father has a big new job with the bank. He has been applying for a transfer for ages and it has finally come through. Ivy said she is going to try to get a job in one of the big department stores because then she will get a store discount on frocks and makeup. She is only seventeen but she looks older especially when she wears her hair up. Mum says she ought to be careful or she might give some young fellow the wrong idea.

The good thing about Ivy going is that there will be a job at the post office in Nyngan that they'll need someone for and I would be perfect. I could still do the job here for Dad in the evenings and work on the telephone exchange as my main job. I have asked if I can drive the truck into town next week so that I can go to see the postmaster. Mum thought it was a good idea, I haven't told Dad yet.

While I'm there I will have lunch with Ivy and Patsy. It will be like a farewell for Ivy and in the future I might be able to visit her in the city. That would be fun.

I have been saving my wages since Christmas and at last I have enough to buy material for a new dress for winter. I saw a picture of Princess Margaret in a magazine. She is so pretty and she was wearing this gorgeous mauve coatdress. I want to find a light wool in that colour and Mum has a pattern that is a similar style. I'll need buttons too, maybe black as a contrast. Patsy has a good eye for dressmaking. I will ask her advice.

Mum had a letter from Kitty yesterday and she and Norm are expecting their second baby any day now. The oldest, Valerie will be just eighteen months. They will have their hands full for a while. She also said that she and Norm have been talking about moving to a bigger town, closer to good schools, less isolated. I hope its not too far from here although even now we don't see them very often. Mum is going to Bourke tomorrow to help with Valerie and be around when Kitty first comes home. Norm works long hours, besides he isn't the type to change nappies or feed babies.

Stella read a few more entries, one announcing that Charlie was engaged and another about her interview at the Nyngan post office which was a success. She started work on the telephone exchange around May and she wrote about how excited she was to be learning to use the new system 'from the inside out', as she put it. There was a more sombre note a few months later.

July 7, 1949

We had a telegram from Norm this morning asking if Mum or I could come and help out with the girls. Kitty is very sick and had to go to the hospital and May is only three months old. Ma has been doing what she can but she is getting too old to look after a toddler and Norm's Mum has a bad heart. Mum thinks it's best if she goes and it's true, she knows more about babies than I do. I think she is worried about Kitty as well. Norm didn't say what was wrong just that she wasn't in any danger. I have only been in my new job for a few months so it's too early for me to ask for holidays anyway.

The new baby, May is very sweet according to Mum. She went up there after she was born to help for a couple of weeks and she said she is the spitting image of Kitty as a baby, all blond curls and blue eyes. Apparently, Valerie is a cheeky one, a real dare devil. Maybe I can drive up to visit for a weekend while Mum is still there. I can stay with Ma and at least I will get to meet the new baby. I will ask Dad if he wants to come as well. He hasn't seen Kitty for ages and she always was his favourite.

The good thing about me not having to go to Bourke right now is that I will be here for the winter ball. It's more of a dance than a ball but it will be fun and Ivy has promised she will come back from Sydney so that we can go together like we did at Christmas. I am dying to hear all her adventures. Patsy had a letter the other day and she thinks Ivy might have a boyfriend in Sydney that she hasn't told us about. I'm not so sure, she is not much good at keeping secrets even by mail. I bet she has the prettiest dress. I'll wear my new dress, it's a bit heavy for a dance but it has a nice, flared skirt and it's a lovely colour.

There were a few more short diary entries about nothing in particular, the usual preoccupations of seventeen year old girls – dances, boys, clothes, work and being allowed to be more independent. Lillian's diary keeping was falling away as her life became busier and there was only one more before that final one about applying for a job in Sydney.

May 1951

Finally I have been at the Nyngan post office long enough to take a long holiday. I plan to visit Kitty and Norm and the girls in the mountains. I have investigated and I can take a train all the way. From there we can do day trips to the city and I can go for walks in the mountain forests. Ivy said she will meet me for lunch one day in the city if I write well in advance. It will be good to spend some time with Valerie and May. I don't know them very well and I haven't seen much of Kitty for ages.

She has been sick again, not needing hospital this time but Norm was worried that all the work of moving house and settling the girls had made her run down.

It will be good for the two of us to spend some time together. I was only fourteen when she left home, still a kid really. It will be different now but she will probably still see me as an irresponsible teenager. Compared to her I suppose she has a point. Last time I saw her after May was born, she was thin and fragile after she had been sick in hospital. She was so pale her skin almost looked blue, like she could shatter at any moment. I hope the mountain air is agreeing with her, putting the roses in her cheeks.

The other reason I am so excited to be taking a holiday because once I get to know the city I can start to make plans for the future. I haven't told anyone yet but I am determined to find a job in Sydney and live away from the family. I need to find out what it's like to live in a place where I can be more than an extension of my family. Mum would say that is selfish thinking and maybe that's true but if I'm not selfish now I will miss my chance.

It was getting late, time for Stella to go to bed after a long week. Still feeling more wound up than she would like she promised herself a hot chocolate as she walked out to check the mail. There was a pile of paper, mostly junk mail that she placed on her balcony table while the milk was heating. The evening was mild for this time of year and the lights on the harbour were particularly beautiful tonight.

Real estate agents wanting to provide a sales estimate, a local plumber looking for business, an electricity bill, nothing of interesting she thought. The bottom envelope had the solicitor's address on the front, presumably a further update on her mother's will. Yes, it was a form to give authority for disbursement of funds to her account, to give disbursement of just under $4 million to her account.

Time to make some choices.

Chapter 26

The hum of students speaking French, English, Italian, the street cleaning truck washing down the road and the smell of bread baking had become familiar breakfast companions. Stella ordered her coffee and croissant, sitting at one of the window tables rather than taking up her usual spot at the bar. After all it was Saturday, a leisurely start to the day was definitely what she needed.

She had been in Paris for three weeks and already she knew that four months of sabbatical would leave her wanting more. Hardly long enough to scratch the surface she thought. Her small apartment above Rue St Jacques was twenty meters from what had become her regular breakfast and sometimes aperitif stopover. She had been immediately charmed by the apartment's eclectic mix of artworks, faux chandeliers, mismatched furniture and grand mirrors. She supposed that this was shabby chic Parisienne style - her landlady certainly came across as a woman of style and substance.

This morning there was the beginnings of a winter chill, not surprising for mid-October but after an Indian summer many people were hugging their torso wishing they had brought a heavier jacket. Stella was looking forward to the change of season, not to mention the chance to wear the beautiful woollen coat she had bought last weekend. A proper winter would be a treat.

Stella had always loved Paris and she had visited many times over the years, never for longer than a week but she had a good grasp of the geography of the city. Her French was awful but fortunately everyone at the University spoke English and were kind enough to translate when needed. She was surprised at how easily she had found her place here, both at the university and in the city.

Of course, the history, the architecture, the fashion, the glamour were fabulous but there was something else as well. French people, Parisians no less, were remarkably helpful and friendly. She knew their reputation and yet her experience refuted all the bad reviews. She was struck by their love of ideas and debate, an appreciation for language and art that was rarely articulated in Australia and a social conscience that pervaded their psyche.

Stella was here after making a snap decision to request sabbatical leave from her university while she wrote up the remainder of her research. Her colleague at the Sorbonne had agreed to sponsor her and her head of school in Australia had been enthusiastic to support her request. Before she knew it, she was applying for a visa and booking tickets and accommodation. Everything had fallen into place quickly.

A laptop and a postcard sat together on the table next to Stella's coffee. She smiled at the paradox, choosing to look at her emails first. She was pleased to see one from Rosemary Benton, hopefully a response to Stella's proposal. When Lillian's estate had been settled, Stella decided she wanted to donate funds towards a program for vulnerable women. It was important to Stella that these funds make a difference and so she had taken what she hoped was a sound business approach.

She asked Rosemary to prepare a case for her consideration within certain broad parameters – the priority would be women at high risk as well as those currently experiencing homelessness. It would be designed specifically for women suffering domestic violence, leaving prison or with mental health problems although a broader scope would be acceptable. Ideally it would be a source of employment for some of these same women – mentors who knew what being homeless was like. She would donate $3 million to the program and this would be the start of a long term program that attracted ongoing funds from other sources.

Rosemary's proposal seemed very thorough and Stella would spend some time over the weekend reading it carefully. She quickly sent a response promising to come back to Rosemary during the following week. It was really happening, elated she thought about all those women who had shared their stories and the countless others who could be helped.

When she had first started to review and analysed the interviews that she collected for her research, Stella realized there were gaps in some of the narratives. Several of the women agreed to a second and even third interview to add greater depth, the back story so to speak. Stella felt she now had a body of work that would contribute something new to the field, as well as a series of compelling biographies that would help others have a better understanding of homelessness. She had decided to aim for a broader audience and to adopt a style and tone that would reach as many people as possible.

This was a new and exciting departure from her usual academic style.

She had not noticed on first glance at the business case but as she looked at it a second time Stella saw that Rosemary's working title was 'Lillian's Legacy'. It was apt.

She pulled herself away from the screen and let her gaze wander along the street outside. The Renaissance, Haussmann, Art Nouveau facades, randomly assorted, never failed to leave her feeling tranquil. Form over function- she breathed in their translucent light, felt the weight of time while absently pulling pieces off her croissant.

Brushing away the crumbs she found a pen to write on the postcard. She worried about Pete; he was looking sad when she last saw him but she knew he would love getting a postcard from Paris. She told him about her week, her apartment, her colleagues and importantly what she had eaten – she recalled his travel guide to western New South Wales had been made up entirely of food stops. No doubt he would be reassured that she had not been eating frog's legs.

Quickly she sent an email to Anna as well. She and her daughter Claire planned to visit Paris in mid-November and Stella was looking forward to showing them 'her' Paris. She asked if they might be interested in taking a cheap flight to Rome for a four day break. Stella had been thinking of visiting Ivan's village and it would be easier not having to do it alone.

There were a couple of more work emails that needed a response before she shut the machine. She sent an invitation for one of her postgraduate students to Skype on Tuesday to talk about her progress and another to Steve asking if he could look out a reference she knew was in the pile on her desk and which she was having trouble finding online.

The café was becoming busier as lunchtime neared and the pressure of waiting eyes eventually stirred her to get the bill. She dropped the change from her coffee in the cup offered by an old woman, sitting near the café entrance. She was well wrapped in an old blanket but if rain set in as forecast, she would have a long cold night ahead. Stella wondered what her options were here in Paris, how well hostels coped with the growing melting pot of refugees, itinerants and homeless people. Making a mental note to discuss it with her colleagues, she found a few more euros in her bag, hoping to ease tonight's discomfort at least.

By midday, Stella had dropped her things back in her apartment and collected an umbrella before setting out to walk along the Seine. It was becoming a favourite route but today the wind was gusting creating a chop on the water and a chill in her bones. Nevertheless she had that Mona Lisa smile as she walked, loving the beauty, feeling at peace with the world. It was the same feeling she had in Sydney when she saw the sun sparkling on the harbour or a full moon rising over the ocean.

Since she left, she had been able to think more about Lillian's story but with a distance that gave her a new perspective. Of course if she had been a French woman, the story would have been absolutely unremarkable. The overhang of Victorian values in Anglo Australia had a lot to answer for, she thought. When she was growing up, she had felt closest to her Dad, like all teenage girls probably. Now she saw the stamp of her grandfather's family in more than her face as it aged to resemble her mother.

Her grandfather had chased new places, her mother new worlds. And Stella, she seemed always to be looking for new ways of seeing those worlds, new points of view. Pete was right when he called them rootless. So many people talked of connection to place, to country. Here terroir was sacrosanct and her colleagues spoke warmly of their origins both historical and geographic. For Lillian home was a shifting idea, on shuffle, new valued over old.

Not surprising then that for Stella, cities were where she was at home. Textured, ambiguous places where you could lose and find yourself at the same time. Anonymity was their gift to those self-contained enough to appreciate it.

Stella was almost at Quai Branly where she had agreed to meet her colleague, Gabriel. They'd had coffee last week and she was looking forward to seeing the Museum with him. His research included the impact of colonization on modern nations and their culture so he would be the perfect guide with whom to see the collection. And as she had admitted in her email to Anna, he was also pretty gorgeous.

Gabriel's grandparents had migrated to France from Algeria in the 1930s but as he said, he was more French than Algerian and more Parisian than French. He was waiting near the entrance, looking suave with his steely hair, cream polo, jeans and RM Williams boots. Stella grinned and hoped the last was for her benefit. Lillian would have approved of that well groomed hair and the loosely arranged scarf at his neck. Stella caught a self-conscious glimpse as she passed a shop window- she hoped the carefully chosen woollen dress matched his chic.

She knew from their previous meeting that Gabriel was passionate about ideas and an entertaining conversationalist but for the first time in ages she was hoping for more than an expansion in her world view. She felt optimistic that their meeting of minds would develop into something more.

Acknowledgments

Some of the details of Lillian's life have been inspired by anecdotes my mother told me of her childhood in far western New South Wales. However, Lillian's life is not her life and she is not Lillian.

My thanks to Iqbal for your love, patience and support as I worked on this novel and to Paolo for lying quietly at my feet throughout.